TEENAGE FATHERS

□□□□□□□□□□□□

KAREN GRAVELLE
AND
LESLIE PETERSON

JULIAN  MESSNER

JULIAN MESSNER and colophon are trademarks of Simon &
Schuster, Inc. Design by Anne Ricigliano. Manufactured in
the United States of America.
Lib. ed. 10   9   8   7   6   5   4   3   2   1
Paper ed. 10   9   8   7   6   5   4   3   2   1

Library of Congress Cataloging-in-Publication Data

Gravelle, Karen,
    Teenage fathers / Karen Gravelle and Leslie Peterson.
        p.   cm.
    Includes bibliographical references and index.
    Summary: Explores various aspects of teenage father-
hood through the experiences of thirteen teenage fathers.
    1. Teenage fathers—United States—Juvenile literature.
    2. Teenage fathers—United States—Psychology—Juvenile
literature.   3. Teenage fathers—Services for—United
States—Juvenile literature.   [1. Teenage fathers.]   I.
Peterson, Leslie.   II. Title.
HQ756.G64   1992
306.85'6—dc20   91-29670
                                                                  CIP
                                                                   AC

ISBN 0-671-72850-4   (lib. bdg.)
ISBN 0-671-72851-2 (pbk.)

Contents

Introduction

Although much has been written about teenage mothers, there is surprisingly little published about the experience of parenthood from an adolescent male's point of view. Unfortunately, what is available focuses primarily on teenage fathers as impregnators— often portraying them as careless, irresponsible, and motivated by a desire to prove their manhood.

Is this what teenage fathers are really like? How do these young men actually feel about becoming parents? What role, if any, do they want to play in their children's lives? How does a teenage father's relationship with his child's mother influence his willingness to become involved with the child? What happens when the child gets older?

By giving young men a chance to talk about their feelings and experiences, *Teenage Fathers* attempts to answer some of these questions. The thirteen young fathers whose stories are presented here demonstrate a wide range of responses to parenthood. A few appear to fit the stereotype of irresponsible young men, wanting little to do with their children. In contrast, others are devoted fathers, truly enjoying both their children and the experience of parenthood. Many fall somewhere in between, struggling against significant obstacles to be the kind of fathers they want their children to have.

As a group, these young fathers reflect the racial and ethnic composition of the United States, with black, white, and Hispanic

Name	Current Age	Age When Girlfriend/ Wife Became Pregnant	Number of Children
Carlos	19	12 to 19	9
Kenton	17	17	Expecting first child
Alex	17	16 and 17	Expecting first child
Joey	22	16 and 18	2
John	18	17	1
Calvin	22	18, 21, and 22	2; expecting third child
Aaron	39	17	1
Raymond	21	19	1
Wayne	22	19	1
Patrick	19	18	1
Gerard	21	15, 18, and 21	2; expecting third child (plus stepson)
Malcolm	22	18	1
Brian	25	18 and 21	2

men represented about equally. Some of them come from inner-city neighborhoods; others live in suburban areas.

Although all the fathers had children during their adolescence, not all of them are teenagers now. Since being a father does not usually stop after a young man enters his twenties, we wanted to explore the experiences adolescent fathers have as they and their children grow older. Thus, some of the men who have contributed to the book are now in their twenties and thirties.

Finally, because we wanted these young fathers to be able to speak freely, we have changed their names. Everything else—their thoughts, feelings, and experiences—has remained untouched.

PART ONE

■

Taking Off

What is it that makes one young man willing to accept the responsibilities of being a father, while another disappears from sight before his child is born?

Of the thirteen teenage fathers interviewed for this book, three had no interest whatsoever in having a relationship with their children. Although the attitudes of the three young men differ in several respects, they also have much in common.

Not surprisingly, one of these features is their age. Although Carlos is now nineteen, his first child was born when he was only twelve years old. Alex was sixteen when his girlfriend first became pregnant, and Kenton was seventeen. Of course, many older adolescents, as well as fully grown men, have been known to disclaim responsibility for their offspring. Still, even under the best of circumstances, it is hard to imagine what kind of father a twelve-year-old boy could possibly be.

Now older, Carlos continues to father children in whom he has no interest, illustrating that age is certainly not the only factor involved in determining what kind of father a person will be. Nevertheless, with the exception of Carlos, the eighteen- and nineteen-year-old adolescents interviewed seemed much more willing and able to take an active role as fathers than did those who were younger.

Another thing the three young men in Part One have in common is their attitude toward sex. As many counselors who work with teenagers have pointed out, adolescent males and females make very different assumptions about sex. Teenage girls typically equate sex with love, while most teenage boys— particularly younger ones—do not. While the girls discussed in this book were not interviewed, there are definite hints that the young women involved with Carlos, Kenton, and Alex had far more emotional involvement in their relationships with their boyfriends than the boys themselves experienced. As most teenage males grow older and develop deeper relationships with their girlfriends, their attitudes toward sex change somewhat, becoming closer to those of teenage girls.

Young men who want little to do with their children also seem to see themselves as having no responsibility in whether or not their girlfriends became pregnant. They feel that if the girl did not want to have a baby, she should have taken some kind of precaution. Her failure to do so, in their minds, indicates that she was not only willing to have a child but to assume full responsibility for it. As an extension of this attitude, they also feel that if they are not living with the mother of their child, they owe neither her nor their child financial support.

Although these young men unfairly expect their girlfriends to assume a greater share of responsibility, their attitude seems to be in part an effort to compensate for another, more subtle, disadvantage they feel they experience. Like some of the teenage fathers who did assume responsibility for their children, Kenton and Alex express resentment of the power they feel young women have to control their lives—a power they do not feel is reciprocal. While it is true that, by taking responsibility for birth control, both boys and girls can share equally in the decision to become or not to become parents, it is also true that girls are better able to deceive males into thinking they are taking precautions when they are not.

Moreover, because of their greater investment in the relationship, adolescent girls occasionally become pregnant in an effort to maintain contact with their boyfriends or to force a greater commitment from them. As Malcolm's story painfully illustrates, Kenton is not the only young man interviewed who feels his girlfriend lied or tricked him into parenthood.

This power imbalance is most obvious in the area of abortion. Regardless of what the young man may want, the decision to terminate a pregnancy is ultimately in the hands of his girlfriend. Since she is the one who will have to undergo pregnancy and delivery, the decision to do so should be hers. Nevertheless, in choosing whether or not to have an abortion, she need not—and often does not—take his wishes into consideration. For an adolescent male struggling to gain independence from the control of adults, feeling that he is now under the thumb of his girlfriend can be a particularly difficult experience.

Finally, none of these three young men grew up with a model of what a father should be. Since boys learn to be parents by observing how their own fathers behave, the absence of a father (or of any other male who takes an extended interest in him) places a young man at great disadvantage in becoming a responsible parent himself. As some of the teenage fathers interviewed later in the book illustrate, this obstacle can be overcome. But, while it is not accurate to say that a boy must have an adequate male role model in order to become a good father, not having one certainly makes the task more difficult.

CHAPTER

1

□

Carlos

"I'm not really the father because I never wanted to be the father."

*A*t nineteen, Carlos is a study in contrasts. Overweight, sloppy, with badly pocked skin and a missing front tooth, he is the least attractive of the thirteen young men interviewed. Yet, unlike most of the others, he seems to see himself as irresistably alluring to women. Since his first child was born when he was only twelve, Carlos is also the youngest teenage father in the book. And, as the father of nine, he has far more children than any of the other men interviewed.

But it is the extreme attitudes he expresses and his total disconnection from his children that differentiate him most from the other teenage fathers interviewed. Perhaps this is partly a result of cultural differences. Carlos has lived in the United States for only a few years, having immigrated here when he was sixteen from a small village in South America. Since he barely speaks English, it may also be hard for him to express how he

5

really feels. As a result, his statements may appear to be more exaggerated than he intends.

What he does say, however, provides some clues as to why Carlos feels and acts the way he does. In many respects, he seems to be repeating a pattern set by his own father and the other men he observed while growing up. "My father had lots of women and a wife too," Carlos states. Although he thinks his parents lived together briefly when he was a baby, after awhile, his father returned home to his wife.

"My mother had many men too," he adds, "and a lot of babies. There were thirteen kids—not the same father. It's different in those small villages," he explains. "Not like here, you know."

When he was eleven or twelve, Carlos began having sex with one of the girls in a group of children he played with. Although she was only twelve as well, Carlos claims her parents weren't upset when she became pregnant. "It wasn't unusual," he states simply.

His girlfriend wasn't supposed to have intercourse imme-diately after having the baby, but she and Carlos ignored this advice. When she quickly got pregnant again, Carlos became the father of two.

Shortly after the baby was born, Carlos and his girlfriend found other partners. His new girlfriend soon became pregnant with his third child.

When asked why he stopped seeing his first two children, Carlos becomes annoyed. "I don't like that you say they are my children," he says. "They have mothers. I'm not really the father because I never wanted to be the father. It just happens because you're young and you have to have sex. But I don't think of them as my kids."

Over the next few years, Carlos fathered many other children as well—eight all together, he thinks. "The girls told me or my friends, but I've never seen them," he says. Carlos doesn't think of these as his children either. "If the girl gets pregnant, then they are hers. That's the way my people are," he explains.

Last year, however, things changed. When his girlfriend Inez became pregnant, she and Carlos started living together. The experience seemed to agree with him. "I was never with a woman, living together and all, before," he says. "She took care of me. I liked it."

Carlos decided to settle down, even buying a TV so that he would stay home more. Although he didn't plan to marry his girlfriend because "you need money for a wife and a baby and I don't get paid too much," he did think of purchasing some furniture. They planned to have Inez's mother care for the baby, since he and Inez would have to continue working.

The relationship didn't last that long, however. Shortly before the child's birth, Inez returned home from work early and discovered Carlos with another woman. Furious, she threw his things in the trash and kicked him out of the apartment.

Carlos claims he was happy with Inez. "But I was getting a little bored. She couldn't have sex [because she was pregnant], so what was I supposed to do?" he asks.

When his daughter, Elena, was born, Inez tried repeatedly to contact him. "She was calling every day after the baby was born," he says. His pride stung, Carlos refused to speak to her. "If she called when I was home, I'd tell her to stop calling or I'd hang up on her. To teach her a lesson," he adds.

It doesn't seem to occur to Carlos that Inez may want him to take some financial responsibility for their child even though they are no longer together. Instead he assumes that she wants to take him back.

For Carlos, however, the baby appears to be merely an extension of Inez. If he doesn't want the mother, why would he care about the child? He doesn't seem to see his daughter as an individual in her own right, much less as someone for whom he should take responsibility.

"I'm not with her mother now," he says, when asked about Elena. "I'm not part of them anymore. Inez threw them [his obligations to his daughter] out when she threw me out. It's as plain as that."

In fact, Carlos gets angry at the suggestion that he should help Inez support his daughter. "Do you think I'm crazy?" he asks. "I don't live with her but I'm supposed to give her money? Only movie stars give money to women like that! I'm not rich and I'm not stupid to do something like that."

Carlos has no plans to see his daughter. "Only if Inez takes me back," he states. Carlos would be willing to reconcile with Inez because she's pretty and treated him well. In fact, he might even be willing to marry her. "But I will always have girlfriends because I am a man," he emphasizes. "If she understands that, maybe I would get married."

Given that Inez threw him out because he was cheating on her, it is hard to imagine that she would go for an arrangement like this. But Carlos doesn't seem to feel that she has too many other options. "She needs me. I can give her things and the baby things that she can't get by herself because she doesn't have enough money."

Perhaps more to the point, he doesn't think that other men will want her now, at least in terms of a committed relationship. "She has my kid," he says, "so she's my woman and she always will be. What man wants someone else's woman?"

Thus, for Carlos, a woman is always bound in some way to the father of her child, while a man doesn't—and, in fact, shouldn't—experience a reciprocal tie. According to Carlos, men who feel responsibility toward a woman come under her control and lose their manhood. "You have to be smart and strong and you don't let the woman hurt you or tell you what to do," he says emphatically. "When the woman tells you what to do, you become like a girl, you lose your soul. It's over!"

Not only does Carlos seem unable to see his children as individuals who are separate from their mothers, but he also appears to have difficulty viewing women as separate from the men that impregnate them. To him, fathering children is a way of branding a woman as belonging to him. As long as he holds attitudes such as these, it will be very hard for Carlos to love anyone—either his girlfriends or his children—even if he wanted to.

CHAPTER

2

□

Kenton

*"It's not like I'm the first guy in history that got
accused of being the daddy when he wasn't.
Everyone says I shouldn't get suckered into this.
And I won't either!"*

A high school dropout, Kenton works in the kitchen of a large
catering establishment. Tall and solidly built, he is physically
impressive. In a strange way, however, Kenton's personality
seems out of place in his body. Although engaging, he comes
across as very young and somewhat effeminate. And very scared.

Michelle, a girl he dated briefly, claims he is the father of the
child she is about to have. Because he had sex with her only
twice, Kenton doubts that the child is his. Instead, he thinks the
young woman is lying in an effort to trap him into taking
financial responsibility for the baby. And he is determined not to
let that happen.

Since it's unclear whether or not Michelle was seeing
anyone else, it's hard to say if Kenton's suspicions are justified or
if he is merely trying to deny responsibility. In spite of the fact

11

that there is at least some possibility that he could be the father, Kenton claims his mother supports his position. "I already told my mom," he says, "and she says if it's not mine, I don't have to do anything." From what he says, it appears that his statement that the child is not his is proof enough for her.

Meanwhile, Kenton is being very careful not to do anything that might later incriminate him. When Michelle first told him she might be pregnant and asked him to take her to the doctor, Kenton refused to get involved. "I don't think I should. I wasn't sure it was my baby and my friends said that as soon as I started to do stuff like that I would have to marry her," he recalls. "And I'm too young for that!"

Nor does he intend to visit her and the child after the baby is born. "As soon as I do something like that, people are going to start talking, and then I'm going to have to start taking care of things. No thanks!"

Even if the baby is his, the suggestion that he should assume responsibility for it angers him. "So what if it is mine?" he asks belligerently. "I didn't ask her to get pregnant! What am I going to do? I'm only seventeen and I don't have a job yet. I'm still in school, sort of, and it doesn't make sense."

Kenton readily admits that the idea of being a father scares him to death. "Of course, it does! Do you know what kind of responsibility it is? What kind of money you need? I think Pampers cost five dollars a box. I don't make that kind of money," he adds. "I live with my mother still. I'm supposed to go back to school too…"

Not only is Kenton overwhelmed at the idea of being a father, but he obviously has very little concept of what fatherhood actually means. His own father disappeared when he was a child. As far as Kenton is concerned, he and his mother are better off without him.

"He was like most fathers, you know? Out for themselves.

I'm glad he's gone," Kenton continues. "He wasn't around and when he was he was beating on my mom."

A good father, in Kenton's eyes, is someone who has a job and isn't a drug addict. "He has to go home everyday...and be nice to his wife and kids. He can't hit them because they make him angry or something."

Although Kenton feels he might want to get married and have children when he's older, he doubts he'll be a good father even then. "I don't think I could," he says. "I think I'd screw it up because I've already hit Michelle and I've hit other girls too."

He regrets having struck Michelle, but thinks he was justified. "She lied and said I was the father of this baby," he explains. "That's a lie and she knows it. I know you're not supposed to hit a girl, but when they start to lie about you, you have to quiet them up. That's what I did. I'm sorry I did that," he adds. "But see? I don't think I'm ever going to be the father of anybody. Not a good father anyway."

In spite of his efforts to disassociate himself completely from Michelle and her situation, Kenton may feel more empathy for her than he acknowledges. "There is a part of me that's concerned, just for her as a human being," he admits. "I hope she finds somebody to take care of her. If I were older and...I don't know."

More than anything, however, Kenton wants to flee—to be far away from the unrelenting pressure of what seems like an enormous and unfair burden. "I wish there was something I could do but there isn't. All I can do is wait this thing out," he says miserably. "I hate this! I wish I could just leave."

Counselors who work with adolescent males say that Kenton's reaction to being told he has made someone pregnant is not at all uncommon. Like him, many young men who have had only a casual relationship with the girl in question believe she is either lying or so promiscuous that it's impossible to identify the male responsible.

However, while Kenton may genuinely doubt that he is the father, that isn't really the issue, since there are tests that can be done to determine paternity. What is more important is the fact that, even if he is the father, Kenton wants nothing to do with the situation. This feeling may be at the bottom of many young men's claim that the girl is not telling the truth.

CHAPTER
3

□

Alex

*"I really don't want to be the father of this baby.
I'm too young! I've got my life ahead of me. I'm
going to blow it all now? I don't think so!"*

With his dramatic good looks and shy, soft-spoken manner, it is easy to see why girls are attracted to Alex. He'd like to go out with some of these young women, but since his girlfriend, Jana, is expecting any day, he doesn't think it would be a good idea right now.

This is the second time since Alex started going out with Jana that she has become pregnant. The first was about a year ago, when he was sixteen. At the time, Jana had an abortion. "She was only fourteen," he says. "She didn't want anyone to know. Her parents would have killed her!"

Alex was definitely in favor of her ending the pregnancy. "We both said an abortion was the way to go. We didn't talk a lot about it because we knew what we had to do," he recalls. Aside from taking part in the decision, Alex had no further involvement in the process. A girlfriend accompanied Jana to the clinic.

15

Alex would have liked Jana to get an abortion this time as well, but she balked at the idea. "She didn't want another abortion," he says. "Her friends told her she wouldn't be able to have any babies if she had another abortion. I told her that was bull but she didn't want to take the chance."

Although it is certainly possible that Jana was worried about her ability to have children in the future, there may have been other factors involved in her decision as well. For example, it appears that she is far more interested in a long-term relationship with Alex than he is.

"Jana talks about living together or getting married in the future," he says, "but I don't know what I'll be up to in a couple of years. Maybe I won't even be here. Maybe I'll move to L.A. I've got family there. I figure I could save some bucks and move out there, you know? It's beautiful there."

He still loves Jana, but, as he says, the feeling is wearing off. "It's not like when I first fell in love with her. Things change after awhile, at least for me. It's gotten a little tired. I'd like to date other girls now," Alex adds, "but that wouldn't be too cool."

He continues to spend a lot of time with Jana, however. "I see her about every other day," he says. "We meet and do something. I don't go to her house or anything, because basically I don't want to be killed. And there are some guys who live on her block that I don't get along with either."

It is obvious that Jana's family is not too happy with either the situation or Alex. "They're upset, of course." he admits. "But they don't want us to get married, so they're not throwing her out or anything."

Instead, they have pretty much taken over, leaving Alex on the outside. As he explains, "It's going to be her kid—*their* kid." Alex has no idea whether Jana has even been to the doctor. Nor does he plan to be at the hospital when the child is born. "Her parents will be there," he says. "Jana knows I'm not going. She understands." Needless to say, the baby's last name will be Jana's.

When asked if he feels left out of the whole process, Alex

answers, "A little, because I am." But if this makes him angry, it is also a big relief. "I'm OK with it," he says. "I'm relieved about it. I didn't want to get married, so it's OK."

Alex's parents are also upset, but for different reasons. "My mom says Jana's a no-good mother because she thinks she is a druggie." Alex denies this. "She doesn't do crack, if that's what you mean. She does a little blow now and then, we smoke…no big deal. But is she a druggie? No way!"

Alex isn't worried that Jana's drug use might hurt their baby. "They say that to scare you," he claims. "It's not one hundred percent true. My aunt did a lot of drugs and her kids are OK. Hey, you know, it's her life, right?" Alex adds. "What am I going to do anyway?"

Alex's father, on the other hand, is glad Jana's family has taken charge of things, evidently because he doesn't think much of his son's ability to handle parenthood—or anything else, for that matter. "He hates my guts!" Alex says angrily. "He blames me for everything. He says I'm no kind of a father, so I guess he's happy with the arrangements."

According to Alex, his father has never liked him. "He's a jerk, he just is! I can't do anything right for him. He's a lousy factory worker and he thinks he's better than me. When I was little, he used to beat the crap out of me—for anything!" he continues. "I hate him! That's why I'm going to move to L.A. I just can't take him anymore! He'll probably throw a party when I leave!"

What kind of father does Alex think he'll be himself? "With this one?" he asks. "Probably nothing."

Although he has vague plans for providing some financial support in the distant future, as a seventeen-year-old high school dropout with a menial job, he doesn't expect to do so now. "When I can start contributing toward the kid I will. I'll try to give Jana some money for college and stuff," he says. "I can't right now, but when I can, I will."

Alex doesn't think that he'll be likely to get more involved in the baby's life when he's older and more ready for parenthood. He suspects it will be too late to form a relationship with the child then. Somewhere down the line, however, he thinks he might want to have other children. "Some day I might have kids and then I'll be good to them," he says, adding, "I won't hit them."

Although Alex gives the impression of being unconcerned and unaffected by impending fatherhood, this facade starts to slip somewhat when he tries to give advice to other young men. Underneath his cavalier exterior, Alex seems to be more upset than he lets on. "Don't get your old lady pregnant!" he says emphatically. "It changes your whole life from what you thought it was going to be. It all changes! I didn't think I would be a father at my age and now I can't do anything about it."

As much as he wishes Jana had gotten an abortion this time too, Alex doesn't really feel comfortable about that as an option either. "I know other guys like me. Most of their old ladies got abortions," he says. "But then you know you killed your kid because you didn't use birth control."

He also resents the control parents and girlfriends have over his life. Although he is definitely relieved to have someone else accept the responsibility for his child, part of him feels that others made all the decisions regardless of what he wanted. "I can't be a father even if I wanted to," Alex comments, "because it looks like parents make you do what they want anyway."

Like Kenton, Alex suspects girls of lying or tricking their boyfriends into parenthood. "Boys shouldn't get too tied down to one girl," he advises. "That's how you get into trouble. Chicks that don't love you make sure they don't get pregnant. The ones that want to marry you are the ones that make themselves get pregnant." It is fairly obvious that he considers Jana to be one of these girls.

Unlike Carlos and Kenton, Alex does acknowledge that boys have an equal responsibility to use birth control. "But how do you know she's not lying?" he asks. "Or she just wants to have sex and doesn't care if it's the wrong time?" He admits that he isn't crazy about condoms, but points out that many girls object to them as well. "They kind of kill the feeling, if you know what I mean," he says. "But it's not just me talking, it's girls too. They hate them!"

What seems to sum up the experience for Alex, however, is his closing statement. "You know, it makes you feel like an idiot. I mean, on the one hand you feel like a man and then you feel like a baby because you don't have any control over what's happening." "It's tough!" he exclaims.

Alex's story is a good example of the different expectations teenage boys and girls often have when it comes to sex. Although it may be unfair to guess what was going on in Jana's mind, the choices she's made and the things she wants suggest that she sees sex as a way of building a deeper relationship with Alex, one that eventually involves their living together as a couple, or perhaps even getting married.

For Alex, sex is just that—sex. At this stage of his life, he is far more involved in breaking away from his family's control and establishing his own independence. Although he cares about Jana, he clearly has no intention of exchanging his freedom for the responsibilities of being either a father or a husband. Thus, if Jana hoped to build a family, she's succeeded—unfortunately, however, Alex is not likely to be part of it.

PART TWO

■

Struggling Against the Odds

Although the three young men described in Part One have a number of things in common, the teenage fathers in Part Two present a much more diverse picture. As a group, they share only two similarities: all acknowledge their children and are interested in having at least some contact with them; and, for a variety of reasons, all are experiencing (or have experienced) real problems in being fathers.

Joey and (as a young man) Aaron fall short essentially because they are not (or were not) trying. Although both men said they love their children and maintained at least periodic contact with them, neither had any interest in doing the real work of parenting.

Aaron is now in his late thirties and his approach to fatherhood has changed. But in his teens and early twenties, he was too preoccupied with establishing his identity as a carefree rebel and shoring up his shaky self-esteem to involve himself in his son's development. Similarly, Joey's self-image as a rap singer and lady's man allows no room for the unglamorous, freedom-restricting aspects of fatherhood.

As Aaron has matured, he has become a concerned, responsible parent. This process has taken a long time, however, and Aaron's son is now a young man in his twenties who resents his father's belated attempts to be a parent. It is possible that, over the years, Joey will develop into a more committed father as well—although he may have to change some of his attitudes and beliefs before this happens.

In contrast, John, Calvin, and Raymond want very much to be fathers in the full sense of the word. For these young men, providing financial support for their children is a major part of performing that role. Unfortunately, all three are poorly equipped to do this. With little education or skills, they are seriously handicapped in their ability to earn a living.

Like these young men, many teenage fathers, particularly in inner-city neighborhoods, are high school dropouts. To get a legitimate job, they must go back to school. Not only can this be hard on their egos, but it means that they must forego earning money until they graduate. Many find this sacrifice very difficult, especially when illegal means of earning money, such as selling drugs, are easily available.

Interestingly, the girlfriends of John, Calvin, and Raymond all exerted a strong influence on them, in each case successfully encouraging them to quit selling drugs and go into a job training program. In Raymond's case, his relationship with his girlfriend has been instrumental in helping him to grow and mature in other ways as well.

The negative side of these relationships is that any stress between an adolescent father and his child's mother can be a stumbling block in his relationship with his child, sometimes disrupting or even severing it completely. Although this certainly occurs with older couples as well, the different expectations that male and female adolescents have of their relationships often lead to disappointment and anger. Of the thirteen teenage fathers interviewed for this book, two—Calvin and Gerard—have had to struggle to remain connected with their children when relationships with the children's mothers fell apart.

The young men in Part Two varied in respect to the roles their fathers played in their lives. While John and Aaron grew up with a responsible father or stepfather in the home, the other three—Joey, Calvin, and Raymond—all had absent, abusive, or rejecting fathers. Calvin and Raymond, like several of the fathers in Part Three, are evidence that some young men can overcome this obstacle and learn to be concerned fathers on their own.

Finally, although it is relatively easy to predict the kinds of relationships the teenage fathers in Parts One and Three will have with their children five years from now, it is very difficult to say what will happen with the fathers (excluding Aaron) described in Part Two. Will Joey mature as Aaron did? How successful will John, Calvin, and Raymond be in finding legitimate employment that will enable them to support their children? Only time will tell.

CHAPTER

4

□

Joey

"My music is me! It has to come first. Everyone knows that, even my ladies."

*I*n many ways, twenty-two-year-old Joey has much in common with Carlos, Kenton, and Alex. But there are important differences as well. For one, Joey married the mother of his children.

Not that he *wanted* to, however. When his girlfriend told him she was pregnant, he was anything but happy. "I liked Marie a lot," Joey recalls, "but I liked other girls too. So when she told me, it really blew me away."

At sixteen, Joey wanted no part of parenthood. He tried to talk Marie into getting an abortion, but she refused. "She said it was a sin," he explains, "that it was killing. I didn't want to get married and have a baby, but she did," Joey continues, "and the pressure was on from her mother." His mother agreed, leaving him little choice. "I knew it wasn't going to work out," he remembers. "I knew I'd be out of there, but what was I going to do? Everyone told me I had to get married, so I did."

25

Joey and Marie moved in with Marie's mother. Although Joey had a job after school, his mother-in-law provided most of the couple's financial support. From the beginning, Joey was miserable. "I wanted to die," he says. "Or run away—*far* away. I hated the whole thing!"

The idea of being there when his baby was born was decidedly unappealing to Joey, so, much to Marie's disappointment, he didn't accompany her to the hospital. "I wasn't with Marie when my son was born," he says. "I can tell you because Marie was angry with me for a long time. She still brings it up sometimes when she wants to talk about how bad I am. I wasn't there for my daughter's birth either," he adds, "but what am I supposed to do? I can't have the baby for her. What, I'm supposed to watch her have the baby? Forget it! I'd get sick."

With the addition of a baby, married life became even harder for Joey to tolerate. "I just didn't want to have to be there—the families, everything. I'm not crazy about babies either. They make me nervous. When my son was born—I was still living with my wife—I never got to sleep. That baby just kept crying and crying. It drove me crazy! The whole scene just bothered me."

At times Joey was afraid he'd actually hurt the baby. "I just kept telling myself, 'Don't kill it!'" In order to cope, he'd leave the house. "What do you do? When it got bad, I'd just go hang with some buddies for a couple of days to get away." Shortly thereafter, he moved out entirely.

"Then my wife got a job," he says. "She moved out a little while later—got her own place. I moved back with her a couple of times, but I could never hang out long enough." During one of these periods, the couple conceived a second child, a daughter.

The problem, as Joey sees it, is simple—he's just not the family man type. "I have to be out there. I'm a musician. I can't be home for too long or I go crazy."

Joey admits he's not available much for his son, now five years old, and his daughter, three. But he sees himself as an average father—not too good, but not too bad either. "I'm better than my old man. That's for damn sure!" he says, and in this regard, he's right.

In fact, Joey seems to have turned out better than any of the males in his family. "My father—forget about it—he was never home. I never saw him. My brothers are all drug addicts. All of them have been in and out of jail. My older brother is *still* in jail. I've never been busted and I don't do drugs," Joey adds proudly. "I'm just into my music and my ladies."

Thus, while Joey hasn't provided much in the way of financial or emotional support to his children, he doesn't think he's hurt them either. Unlike his own father, he's never beaten them. And, in his way, he does care about them. "I guess I don't show them too much," he admits. "But I do love them. I'm just not the kind of guy that hangs home with the kids. I never have been."

Given his own childhood experiences, it is not surprising that Joey has little idea of what being a good father entails. "If he loves his kids, right?" he asks. "If he takes them places. You know, if he buys them toys sometimes—stuff like that. I accept that they are my kids," he says, describing himself as a father. "I see them every so often. When I've got money, I'll give them a little. I'm easygoing. I don't get on them a lot. I'm funny with them, I make them laugh. I think I'm generous when I can be—when I can afford it."

Even taking care of his children for a week or two is more day-to-day responsibility than Joey is willing to accept, however. "How would it look," he asks indignantly, "if Joey Calderon didn't play because he had to be with his kids? Me? I mean, forget about it! I have to be out there. I can't be staying home. I'm going to be a star, you know! When I'm rich, then I can take care of things."

Like Carlos and Alex, Joey doesn't think it is unfair that his wife is shouldering the entire burden of caring and providing for their children. As far as he is concerned, if she wasn't willing to do so, she shouldn't have gotten pregnant. "That's why I don't feel so bad about not being around," he explains. "If she didn't want kids, then she should have been on the pill or something. If I were the one who could get pregnant, I'd be on the pill for sure!"

He also rejects the idea that his children may want and need more from him than he is willing to offer. "Kids are used to what they have," he says. "I've never been a 'Father Knows Best' kind of thing. They know me as the Mad Rapper. Why are they all of a sudden going to want more? If I were like that and then all of a sudden I left town, then they'd miss me. But the way it is is the way they're used to. I mean, everybody's like that."

What does he think his son and daughter will remember about him when they get older and look back? "That I was nice to them, that I'm a famous rap star," he answers, laughingly. "They'll be cool with me. I didn't hurt them or anything." And, for Joey, that's enough.

Although he is twenty-two years old, Joey seems stuck at an earlier stage of development. He treats his wife as if she were his mother and his children as if they were his siblings. Although he doesn't see himself as the "father type," he expects women to take responsibility for his sexual behavior as well as their own and thus is not motivated to insure that he doesn't become a father again.

To Joey's credit, however, he has managed to break the cycle of drugs and domestic violence in which he was raised and has not inflicted that legacy on his children. In this regard, he has done them a great favor!

CHAPTER
5

□

John

*"I enjoy my son! Especially when I put my face
in his stomach and watch him laugh. Oh, man,
that's fun!"*

As the proud father of a seven-month-old baby, John is new to
parenthood. So far he seems thrilled with the experience and
determined to take a role in his son's life. But John faces a
number of obstacles. The least of these is that he appears young,
even for eighteen years old. Far more problematic are his lack of
education and job skills and his prison record. But the biggest
hurdle he will have to overcome is resisting the temptation to
sell drugs again.

Becoming a father seems to have helped John focus his life,
however, and things may be changing for him. He is now in an
employment program for teenage parents. Hopefully, when he
finishes, he'll be able to get an legitimate job that will enable him
to support his son.

Although he feels that becoming a father has been a good
thing, John never expected it to happen so soon. "I didn't want a

kid at that time," he says. "I mean, I didn't *plan* to have it. Now that I have it, I regret saying that. 'Cause having a kid is the best thing in the world!"

Vera, the young woman who was to become his son's mother, lived on his street, but John barely knew her at the time. "It was supposed to be a one-night stand," he recalls. "But she wound up having my son!" Far from being upset, John seems pleasantly surprised that he ended up with her, especially since friends told him that Vera was much too good-looking to be interested in him.

Surprisingly, Vera never came right out and told John she was pregnant. "She didn't tell me. I just knew she was pregnant because she wasn't the way she was before she was pregnant," he explains. "She'd eat weird things and she always kicked me out of bed."

Vera's parents were upset at first because she was only sixteen, and John's mother had wanted him to wait until he was twenty-five to have children. Nevertheless, both families seemed to take the situation pretty much in stride.

About the only discussions John and Vera had on the subject were what things they were going to have to get for the baby and what to name it. In terms of the latter, the discussion was very brief. "She had a naming book," John recalls. "I asked her what she got it for, since he was going to be named after his father."

Unlike Joey, John wanted to be present when his child was born. But Vera was in labor for close to thirty hours. Seeing him sleeping, the hospital staff sent him home. "Just after I left, she had the baby," he says with chagrin.

Vera's family moved to another part of the city, so John doesn't see her and the baby as often now. "But when I want him, I go get him," he says. "Most definitely!"

John clearly loves being with his child. "The best thing about being a father is just to go *see* your son! To go see him, walking around in his walker, laughing and giggling, and all that."

He imagines what it will be like when his son is just a little older and able to communicate. "We'll be outside walking around and he'll be like, 'I want this, Daddy,' and I'll *get* it for him! That's the way it was with my stepfather," he adds.

"I want him to *be* somebody," John says. "Not like I was! I'm not saying I was a bad person, because I wasn't. I was a good person till I went to jail. Then that was it! I became a maniac! See, I can't tell his future right now," he continues. "He's still a baby, a little itsy baby. He's not even little yet. Maybe when he gets like twenty months, or something like that, he'll be talking to me and telling me what he wants. That's what I want him to do!"

For John, being able to provide for his son is obviously an important part of being a father. Although John never knew his own father, his stepfather seems to have assumed financial responsibility for him. The man must be a caring person as well, because it is easy to see that John feels great affection for him. "My stepfather, he's the best!" John recalls. "When I wasn't messing up, he'd give me whatever I wanted. I could ask him for a hundred dollars to go get a pair of shoes, or another hundred for something else, and he'd give it to me."

Since he got involved with drugs, however, his stepfather has pulled back somewhat. "But now, he won't…too much stuff I've been doing," John explains. "He trusts me, he just doesn't trust me like he used to."

Although he's determined to support his son, John is beginning to discover how expensive it is to raise a child. "The worst thing about it is all the dough you've got to kick out! For Pampers, clothes…wow! But I don't care!" he adds. "I'll pay the price for anything for my son! I'll do anything for that little boy! It's just that I can't face going back to jail. I can't take that risk."

Avoiding jail means giving up the only way of making money that John has known. "Nowadays, some of these fathers, they're out here robbing and stealing just to get their kids something. I could have done that," John admits. "I could have been doing all of that. But then my son's mom says, 'I don't want you doing that. You can't be living that life no more, doing this and that.'"

John realized that she was right, so when she asked him to go to her social worker for help in getting a job, he went. As a result, he's now in a training program. "Hopefully, I can get a job...making the kind of money drug dealers make," he says. "And not take risks at the same time."

Although returning to school has been difficult for John, he feels it's worth it. "It's worth it to my son, too," he adds. "If he wasn't here, I think I'd be dealing drugs right now."

Like several other young men interviewed, however, John finds himself in an uncomfortable bind. Although Vera is glad that John is in a training program, at the same time, she's unhappy that he doesn't have the kind of money he used to. "She's proud of me," he says, "but she wants it to be *better*. See, before I came here, I was making money. She wants it to be like that again...but she knows once I get into that, there's no stopping me."

John tells her, "I can't do that anymore," and she says she understands. It's clear that Vera is becoming impatient, however, and John definitely feels under pressure. "If things don't go right, though," he acknowledges, "I'll probably go back to dealing drugs."

He tells other teenagers—boys and girls—who have children to use the opportunity to get themselves together. "Take advantage of having a kid so you can stay out of trouble, so you won't get locked up," John advises. "Like, if I want to sell drugs, I won't sell them because I'm thinking about my son. That's a good way to take advantage of your baby."

If John can find a decent job, he may be able to follow his own advice.

For some adolescent males, fathering children may be the only means of defining themselves as grown men. However, unlike the stereotype of the young male who is interested only in siring children, many of these teenage fathers are eager to assume the responsibility of caring for their offspring. Like John, they use the structure provided by the role of parent as a way of focusing their attempts to enter adulthood.

Unfortunately, our society has given young men like John few of the tools necessary to fill the role of father, particularly in terms of being able to support themselves and their families. Without a high level of skills and/or education, the prospects of John ever being able to earn a decent living—much less the kind of living possible from selling drugs—are scant indeed.

6

□

Calvin

"I'm going to be there with all my kids. I don't care if I have a kid here, or one way across town. I'm going to make sure all my kids know their brothers and sisters. Make sure everything is organized and united!"

At twenty-two years old, Calvin is already the father of two children, with a third on the way. Although he wants to be a part of his children's lives, the fact that they are by three different young women makes juggling all the relationships involved difficult. As he's discovered, when the relationship with the mother of one of his children becomes rocky, the casualty can be his relationship with the child.

Calvin moved to the United States from the Caribbean when he was thirteen to be with his mother and sisters. Not long after he turned fourteen, he got into trouble and was sent to a juvenile center for four years. It was here, shortly before he was to be released, that Calvin met Lonette.

Although he was eighteen and she was fourteen, Lonette

appeared much older. "When she told me she was fourteen, I couldn't believe it!" he says. "She had the body of a lady that was seventeen, eighteen years old at the time." In spite of her age, Calvin figured, "Hey we're up here. You're going to need loving and I'm going to need loving so..." As Calvin puts it, "one thing led to another," and Lonette became pregnant.

Far from being uptight about the prospect of becoming a father, Calvin looked forward to it. "I felt *good*," he says, "'cause I was going to be coming home soon. Then when I came home, I went and found a job, so it was cool."

Fortunately for Calvin, Lonette's family liked him. "The only thing that saved me was that her mother and me were real close," he recalls. "Lonette took me to meet her mother and everything, and then when she finally told her at Christmas that she was pregnant, it was all right."

Calvin's mother had a different reaction. She wasn't feeling well at the time the couple told her. "My mother was sick," Calvin recalls "and then I said, 'Ma, Lonette's pregnant.' She was sick and she just got sicker. She was like 'The girl's only fourteen!'" he adds. "But as time when on, it really didn't bother her too much."

The adjustment to parenthood was more difficult than either Calvin or Lonette anticipated, however. For Lonette, having to take care of the baby meant she couldn't hang out with friends anymore. For Calvin, the problems were more financial.

"I was in this program, and they were only paying eighty dollars a week," Calvin explains. "That didn't even cut it! I saved fifty dollars for milk and Pampers. After that, there was nothing but thirty dollars for car fare, clothes...we couldn't live on that! I started selling drugs, and she couldn't deal with it," he continues. "I tried to get her to realize, 'I'm not doing it for me. I'm doing it for you and the baby.' But she couldn't understand that. She was like, 'What happens if you go to jail?' I said, 'I'm not worrying about it. If it happens, it happens. But I got to think of something. How's thirty dollars going to take care of the three of us?'"

When his son, Dannon, was three months old, Calvin and Lonette broke up. "Then I started getting arrested, going to jail. I'd call from jail, telling her 'I want to see my son. Come bring my son up to visit.' But she'd found a new boyfriend, so you know how that went."

Even after eighteen months in prison, Calvin still wanted to see his son. "When I came home, I called her and said I was coming over to see the baby," he says. "She was never there when I came over, so I could meet this guy. I spoke to him while I was in jail over the phone, but I never met him."

Knowing something about the man who lived with Lonette was important Calvin. "Yeah," he says, "because if you're going to claim to be taking care of my baby, I want to see what kind of guy you are. You know, 'cause even if me and her don't have anything going on, I still care for what's mine. I wanted to be sure he was decent," Calvin adds. "That he doesn't mess up and do the same thing I was doing. Because if it's like *that*, then I could be with her and be doing the same thing. I want somebody *better* to take my place. If you're going to be better for her, then don't do what I was doing."

Although Lonette didn't want to be with Calvin any longer she was still concerned for him. "I don't think she wanted me back," he recalls. "But I think she cared and wanted to help." At her encouragement, he enrolled in the special high school she was attending. After five days, he quit.

"I got back into the drug game, and that was it," Calvin recalls. Lonette urged him not to drop out of school. "She was really trying to help me at that time," he admits. "But I said, 'No, I need money, I just came home and I like to wear expensive clothes and everything, you know. I don't like anything cheap!'"

Part of Calvin's behavior seems to have been an effort to get back at Lonette. "I was so stuck up and stubborn and I said, 'It's my turn now. You did it to me, now it's my turn!' But I didn't hurt anybody but myself," Calvin says regretfully. "'Cause if I'd stayed in school then and did what I had to do, I'd have never gone to jail after that. I was arrested after that like eight, nine times. I had to stay in jail all that time, when I could have been out there working right now, working some type of job."

Calvin is in a job-training program now and seems determined to finish. His relationship with Lonette has really suffered in the meantime, however, and this has interfered with his seeing his son.

He knows he has to take the initiative if he wants to see the child, so he does. "I don't wait till she calls me and tells me to come over or whatever. I just call, 'Yo, I'm coming over. I don't want to see you. I don't care if your man's there, or you got company. You can do whatever you want to do, I'm just coming over to see my son.' Sometimes, she gives me a hard time—then sometimes, she doesn't."

"But you know, he barely knows me. Sometimes, I go over there, he'll be asleep, and she doesn't want me to wake him up. I just look at him and leave. And I won't see her or go over there for like another three or four months."

Two and a half months ago, he and Lonette had a serious falling out, and Calvin hasn't spoken to her since. "We had Family Day one day at school, where we brought the kids to the program," he explains. "So I called her up and said, 'Let me bring Dannon.'"

Lonette's response was, "I'm coming too." Calvin didn't want her to come to the school and felt this indicated that she didn't trust him. "I said, 'No, you aren't coming. What do you have to bring him for? That's my son too. I'm going to bring him right back to you when we leave school,'" Calvin recounts. "It's not like I was going to run away with him or something. I'm not going to do that."

When Lonette insisted, Calvin hung up the phone. "I said, 'Forget it! You don't even have to think about it.' And I haven't talked to her ever since then."

Calvin believes Lonette is using the child to get back at him. "I feel hurt!" he says. "Even though we didn't hit it off, why take it out on him?"

His relationship with Kendra, the mother of his second son, is much smoother. In part, he attributes this to the fact that he has been able to provide for the child from the past sale of drugs. "This one, it's all right," he says. "'Cause we've got a little money saved away from drug money and a little bit of money we get from the school." Also, Kendra knows about his relationship with his current girlfriend, Denise, and doesn't make too many demands on Calvin.

The problem is that Denise has no idea Calvin had been seeing Kendra, much less that he has a child by her. He recognizes that he'd better tell her, but feels he may lose her if he does. "See, I want to, but I don't know how to tell her that I've been cheating," he explains.

"But I don't want her to see me one day walking with his mother and we're pushing the baby. Or then she hears in the street from somebody else that I've got another baby. Or she's wondering, 'You left this amount of money in the drawer and I come back and it's gone. What did you do with it?' So before I get into all that, I'm going to have to tell her."

Unfortunately, this is not the first time Calvin has cheated on Denise, and she's let him know that she planned to leave if he did it again. "She told me, 'The next time with another girl, it's over! I don't care what you say or what you do, I gave you *more* than three chances!'"

Calvin feels Denise is special and doesn't want to lose her. "We went through *so much* together!" he says. "She's there for me all around. When I need, she's there. She's not the type of girl that's always running behind a guy for money, money, money. That's the girl for me!"

Calvin is also afraid that Denise, now three months pregnant, may be so disgusted with the relationship that she'll decide to have an abortion. "She might figure, 'Forget this!' and I want to see this baby too," he says. "So I won't tell her until she's like seven months, eight months along."

Or he might wait even longer, until after she has the baby. "'Cause if I tell her now, she's going to want to fight, and I'm not going to *hit* her, you know, 'cause she's pregnant. I want to see my children grow up," Calvin says. "Me, I never had a father. Well, I've got a father but before I was born, he was gone—in jail or something, but he was gone. I see him now," Calvin continues. "To this day, we try to get a little closer, but it's too *late* now! I'm twenty-two years old. What can you possibly tell me? Where were you at when I was ten, eleven, thirteen, fourteen and having trouble? Where were you at then, to prevent all that from happening? I always said to myself, 'When I have kids, that's not going to happen! I'm going to *be* there with all my kids.'"

For Calvin, supporting his children is a major part of fathering. "I want to get into computers, computer programming, or something like that," he says. "If I can't, I'll take anything. I'm not going to be like, 'I don't want to do this, or whatever.' I'll take anything, it doesn't matter. I'll take whatever comes along. Because I've got to take care of my kids, that's mandatory!"

But he clearly wants to know them as well, to share his life with them. "I want to see my kids," Calvin stresses. "Even if me and the mother break up, that's got nothing to do with me and my son or me and my daughter. The only way I'm going to not see my kids is if their mother moves out of state somewhere. And even if they do, I'm going to find my best way to get there at least once or twice a year!"

It is also important to Calvin that his children know each other as well and have some sense of family. "They're going to know their brothers or sisters, regardless," he promises. But, if he intends to stay with Denise, it will be hard for that to happen unless he tells her about *all* his children.

Although Calvin doesn't seem to have difficulty relating to his children, his relationship with their mothers leaves something to be desired—at least in the eyes of two of the young women involved. Unfortunately, Calvin is not the only father interviewed to have had contact with his child disrupted by disagreements with the child's mother. Since this scenario is all too common among older couples, it is no surprise that young men and women with less maturity have difficulty working together as parents when their romantic relationship dissolves. If he is not careful, however, Calvin may be in danger of establishing a pattern in which he alienates the mothers of his children and thereby limits his access to the youngsters themselves.

CHAPTER
7

□

Aaron

*"I should have played a better role in his life. I
didn't, and the shame of it is that I can't make
up those years. The most important years of his
life—and I was brain dead."*

At thirty-nine, Aaron is the oldest of the men whose experiences are presented here. His son is now twenty-one, the same
age Aaron was when he got divorced. Aaron fervently hopes that
his son makes better choices than he did.

As Aaron recalls, his adolescence was one long battle for
acceptance. "I was a fish out of water. I'm white but grew up in a
black and Hispanic neighborhood. It seemed everytime there
was a new kid around, I'd have to be humiliated and terrorized,
even by guys I knew all my life. I was so determined to fit in and
be one of the boys that I'd run right into fists if I had to," Aaron
remembers.

"You know the guy in school who was the nerdy one? The
one everyone had to poke fun at in order to prove their status in
the class?" he asks. "That was me. But I had friends too," Aaron

43

adds. "I could walk down the roughest street and, on a good day, everyone hanging out would shake my hand or slap me on the back. I was a fixture. On bad days, I'd be tarred and feathered if that was the general mood," he admits. "But these guys would also be there for me in a flash. They'd never let anyone from out of the neighborhood get to me."

Then, in what seemed like a stroke of luck, he met Beth. "She was so impressed with my standing in the neighborhood—no kidding—that she almost threw herself at me," Aaron recalls. "She's white too, so I guess she said to herself, 'Well, look at this little guy. He's lived here all his life and he's not dead yet, so…'"

Being with Beth gave Aaron's reputation a boost just when he needed it most. "With Beth, I was a big man. She was the best thing that could have happened to me at that age!" Aaron recalls. "I wasn't going to be tormented about not having a woman or being a faggot, which would have been the natural progression for that crowd. And she made it clear, even for a brief time in my life, that she didn't want anyone else," he adds. Heady stuff for someone who saw himself as an ugly duckling.

Although the couple didn't plan to have a child, when Beth became pregnant, Aaron wasn't upset. For one thing, at seventeen, it provided him with an escape from his parents. "I wanted out of my home and I wanted Beth," he admits. "We'd talked about shacking up together, so this was as good a reason as any."

Besides, it added to his standing in the neighborhood. "Being a father meant you were a man," Aaron comments. "Every other guy had a chick with a baby somewhere. It was definitely a status symbol for a Jewish kid growing up in a black and Hispanic ghetto. I actually felt more like one of the boys."

Assuming the responsibilities of fatherhood didn't worry him. "I was infallible," he says. "I figured I could handle anything."

Both his parents and Beth's wanted them to get married before the baby was born. "But neither of us were the kind that recognize pressure, especially from our families. We were 'rebels,'" Aaron says, laughing.

"But I wanted my son to have my name, as selfish as that sounds, and I was probably a little insecure about our relationship," he adds. "I was always afraid I'd lose Beth to someone else—or to no one else in particular."

As a result, the couple got married right after Joshua was born. "This is going to sound funny," Aaron says, "but Beth didn't want to be pregnant when she got married, so we waited."

The marriage was, in Aaron's words, "the second worst mistake we made." He and Beth fell apart almost immediately.

Unlike many of the teenage fathers interviewed, Aaron and Beth's problems were not financial. "Her family had a lot of money," he says. "We had everything a young couple could need."

Beth just wanted out.

"I was a mess," Aaron says, describing his reaction to the breakup of his marriage. "I thought life as I knew it was over! At first, I fought it," he continues. "I loved her, but she became such a bitch that I finally gave up. She'd obviously made up her mind about it, and there just wasn't any communication anymore. She'd closed the book on me. So what do you do? After you get over feeling like a fool, you decide to go on. It was hard on me because, well, as you can see, I'm not a real attractive guy, and I wasn't much of a looker as a teenager either. I think my worst fear at the time was that I'd never be in a relationship again," he concludes.

The question of custody never came up. "She practically started each sentence with, 'The baby stays with me...'" Aaron continues. "But to be fair, she allowed me to continue a relationship with my son. I've always been in his life. I haven't been much of an influence," Aaron admits. "But what do you expect from a stupid kid who's divorced by the time he's twenty-one?"

In some respects, Aaron viewed his son in much the same

way he had viewed his wife—as someone who made him look good. "I thought Joshua was cute for so many years," he says. "That was the most important thing to me as a young father. I had a cute kid. So I'd take him out and show him off."

Looking back, Aaron thinks he was much too young to be a responsible parent. "If you're seventeen, eighteen, nineteen with a kid, your priorities aren't college funds, encyclopedia sets, or even going to bed at a reasonable hour. When you're that age, you're just breaking free yourself. Your friends, rock 'n' roll, going out, how you look, who's playing at the clubs—that's what's important. No matter how painful it is to admit, your child falls low on the list."

Aaron feels that he set a particularly poor example for his son, and that the lack of a good role model has had a devastating impact on Joshua's development. "It never occurred to me that I would have an impact on who he became. I was a kid—I never thought," he comments. "I wasn't a very responsible person. I never saved money, never had a real home. I was a hot shot photographer, or so I thought. I was a rebel, a carefree jerk," Aaron recalls.

"And that's exactly where Joshua is now," he continues. "But the simple truth is that I was more intelligent at his age than he is. I'm really concerned for him. I can't imagine how he will survive! He has absolutely no motivation because his mother and I have spoiled him. Neither of us taught him how to work for anything, how to go after something. If he wanted something that we could afford, he got it. If he wanted to go somewhere, he went—no questions, no restrictions. We parented as only kids could. It's a shame."

Aaron's relationship with his own father wasn't ideal, but his father was present and provided structure and a set of values for him as he was growing up. "We were never very close," Aaron recalls. "But I can appreciate the basics that he passed on to me. Like, you follow the rules—at home and at school—or you're in serious trouble. My father taught me respect for a lot of things— my elders, teachers, honesty. I did well in school probably only due to the fact that I knew my dad would have kicked the living daylights out of me if I didn't," he acknowledges. "Joshua never had that kind of motivation. I wish I had given him a little more to work with."

Although Aaron feels he has something to offer Joshua now, it's a little late. "Now I'm trying to make an impression on him and, of course, he thinks I'm a jerk," Aaron says. "I can't blame him. I mean, where the hell am I suddenly coming from?"

If Aaron could turn back the clock, what would he do differently? "I wouldn't have had a kid at that age," he says emphatically. "I know it sounds terrible. I love Joshua, but I've done him a great injustice."

Aaron's internal struggles during his teens and early twenties left him particularly ill-suited to be a father. Preoccupied with compensating for his very low self-esteem, he related to his wife and child as accessories that made him feel more acceptable. Rather than seeing Joshua as an individual that needed to be nurtured, Aaron treated him as an object to be displayed.

As the same time, Aaron's need to see himself as a carefree rebel, unencumbered by restrictions, conflicted with assuming any actual responsibility for his son—so he didn't.

Aaron grew up. Unfortunately, by the time he was willing and able to be a real father to Joshua, his son was an adolescent in the midst of rebelling himself.

CHAPTER
8

□

Raymond

*"My father doesn't want his wife to see me. Now
I'm twenty-one and she still doesn't know I'm
alive. And I tell him, 'One of these days, I'm
going to go up to your wife and tell her
who I am.'"*

*I*n some ways, Raymond provides a preview of what Carlos's, Kenton's, or Alex's sons may experience growing up. As the offspring of a sixteen-year-old boy and a twenty-one-year-old woman, he struggles with the fact that his father considers him a youthful indiscretion to be forgotten or swept under the rug. Raymond now has a child of his own. To his credit, his response to parenthood has been very different from his father's.

Raymond first met his girlfriend, Lisa, when she was eight or nine years old. "She was a little girl," he recalls, "and I didn't pay any attention to her. But through the years, I got to talking to her, and we got to be friends, real good friends."

Lisa was thirteen when they started going together. That was four years ago. She and Raymond have been together ever since.

Before Lisa, Raymond had steered clear of romantic relationships. "I'll tell you the truth, I'm a shy guy," he admits. "I made love to girls like four or five times. I never used to be interested. I didn't want them to take my money, to play games."

As a drug dealer, Raymond had plenty of money to take. But unlike other girls, Lisa wasn't particularly interested in it. "I used to throw four, five, six hundred dollars, sometimes two, three thousand dollars on top of the table, and I'd say, 'Baby, you need something, just take it.' 'Cause I used to make a lot of money, you know. But she never touched the money! I'd leave it right on top of the table, and she'd never touch it!" he exclaims. "She'd say, 'Raymond, I'm going to take twenty dollars.' She used to ask me if she could take twenty-dollars," Raymond recounts in disbelief.

"That's what I like about her, that's why I stick with her," he adds. "Because with other girls, if I put that on the table, other girls would just take it."

Lisa is special in other ways as well. For one thing, she is consistently in Raymond's corner. "She'll do anything for me! If I tell her, 'Jump off a roof,' she'll jump off a roof. That's the way she is. She's like no one else."

Raymond began supporting Lisa years ago, even before she had his child. "Her mother used to buy her clothes," Raymond says. "The minute her mother knew I took her virginity away, she never used to buy her no more clothes, never used to give her money. But I love the girl very much, you know," he continues. "So I said, 'Forget it! If her mother isn't going to do it, I'll do it.'"

Given Raymond's background, it is amazing that he has been able to develop the capacity to care for others and to take responsibility for them, since no one seems to have taken care of him, even as a small child.

As a youngster, Raymond and his mother lived with Raymond's older sister. "My sister had a problem with my mother, so she threw my mother out of the house," Raymond recounts. "After my mother had bought everything for the house, she threw my mother out. I was about ten years old, so I couldn't do anything. I was just a little kid. We started living with friends, in other people's houses, but I was really confused," he adds. Eventually, his mother took him back to his sister, while she went to live elsewhere.

Although he had a place to sleep, from this point on, it appears that Raymond was pretty much on his own. "I was in the streets," he says, speaking of his childhood. As a juvenile, he was used as a drug carrier. When he was twelve, he began selling drugs, first pot, then cocaine, heroin, and crack. Raymond was never involved in drugs himself—it was simply a means of making money.

"I give myself credit," Raymond says, "because through all those years, I never took drugs. I hated dope fiends, people that used drugs. I used to sell drugs to them, but that's the way I used to make my money. Just like stores, I figure I'm just selling drugs the same way, trying to make a living."

When, at nineteen, Raymond found he was going to be a father, he was happy and excited. Since Lisa is a diabetic, however, she was worried the baby would be born with problems. "She thought the baby was going to come out little," Raymond recalls. "I used to tell her, 'The baby's not going to come out little, believe me!'"

To make sure that didn't happen, Raymond concentrated on seeing that Lisa ate a lot. "When she was pregnant, I used to be feeding her every day, morning, afternoon, and night," he says. "I told her, 'The baby's going to come out fat.' And the baby came out eight pounds nine ounces. For a diabetic, that's pretty big!"

He also attributes the baby's good health to the fact that he didn't use drugs. "Because if she was using insulin, and I was using drugs, the baby would have come out small," he states.

The birth of his daughter altered Raymond's life dramatically. For one thing, it changed how Lisa felt about his selling drugs. "Before the baby, I was selling drugs and at that time it didn't bother her," Raymond says. "She didn't have a kid, so it didn't bother her. She was free, I was free, so I could do what I wanted to do. When the baby was born, I was still selling drugs, for like another month, because I needed money to buy everything—Pampers, a crib, all that stuff. I told her, 'After tomorrow, I won't sell anymore.' And I kept on selling, and I said, 'Two, three more months.' And she told me. 'It's either the drugs or me. What do you want to do?'" Raymond agreed to stop, but after awhile he started selling pot again. "More quietly, but it still was the same thing," he admits.

Lisa wants him to get a job, but for Raymond, like many other young fathers, that is easier said than done. Because of his chaotic childhood, Raymond never finished high school. In addition, he has a prison record. He is back in school now, however, hoping to become a computer technician or, preferably, a private investigator.

In the meantime, he and Lisa are having real trouble adjusting to the drastic drop in their income. The training program in which Raymond is enrolled pays very little money, not nearly enough to enable him to get an apartment for himself, Lisa, and his one-and-a-half-year-old daughter. As a result, Lisa and the baby are staying with her family.

"Right now, she's living with her mother and brothers, and there are seven people living in the same house, a four-room apartment. She's sleeping on the floor with the baby," he says. "I feel sorry, you know. I don't think it's good for the baby."

It's also making Lisa miserable. "She cries to me everyday, 'I want to leave! I want to be with you!' But I tell her, 'I'd rather see you here than be in the street.'"

Pressured on the one hand to stay away from illegal activities and on the other to support his family, Raymond is near the end of his rope. "It's getting hard!" he says in frustration. "If I was selling drugs out there, you know how fast I could find an apartment? But she doesn't want me to sell drugs. Sometimes I feel like going back out there," he admits, "at least to make the money for the apartment—the first payment."

Raymond's efforts to take care of Lisa and his daughter are in stark contrast to his own father's behavior. Raymond's father was sixteen and his mother twenty-one when Raymond was born. Two years later, the couple separated. For awhile, his father sent child support for Raymond, but he never came to see him.

Raymond vividly remembers the day his mother sent him to meet his father. "My sister took me," he recalls, "and I was all dressed up. My mother had bought me a nice suit to go meet him." The meeting was a disaster. "He rejected me, told me he didn't want to see me," Raymond recounts painfully. "I was about six or seven, and he rejected me."

A few years later, Raymond tried again. When his father denied that Raymond was his son, Raymond became furious. "I said, 'What do you mean, I'm not your son? If I wasn't your son, why did you put your name on my birth certificate?' Plus, I look like the guy!" Raymond adds.

"He was sixteen then, so he's telling me he didn't know what he did. I said, 'You made me, you created me, so I'm here now! You can't change that. The only way you can change that is by killing me, but I guess you don't have the heart to do it.'"

To add salt to the wound, Raymond's father has married and established a second family. Raymond believes his father's three daughters receive a great deal of love and affection from their (and his) father. "Yeah, he treats his other kids good. I don't know why he treats me like this. Now he has three girls and I don't even know them. He's been trying to have a boy. He told me once that he wanted a boy. 'I'm the only boy here!' I said."

Not only does Raymond's father refuse to have anything to do with him, but he hides Raymond's existence from his wife and daughters. Raymond thinks that one reason for this is the ethnic difference between them. Raymond's father is of southern European descent and his mother is Puerto Rican, and Raymond has his mother's darker complexion.

"Yeah, that's the problem," Raymond sighs, "he thinks Puerto Ricans go around robbing people, but I'm not like that. I used to tell him, 'I'm not like everybody else. I could have robbed you a long time ago. The cops aren't going to do anything because I'm your son.'"

Raymond is painfully aware how different his life would have been if his father, who is now wealthy, had taken an interest in him. "People tell me, 'Why you got a rich father and you don't do something with your life?' And I tell them, 'If he would have given me a chance, I would have done something. If I'd been with him, maybe I could have been a success in life.'"

In spite of the constant rejection he has experienced, Raymond still tries to find ways to connect with his father, if not by having a relationship with him, then at least by identifying with him. Ironically, one thing he thinks they share in common is that, like him, Raymond's father treats his children well—the children that matter, that is.

Raymond's relationship with Lisa is unquestionably the most stable in his experience. To him, she has always represented family. Although they aren't legally married, he thinks of her as his wife and refers to her as such. "Ever since the first day," he says, "she's been my wife. I told her, 'You're going to be mine.' I care more about my wife than anybody."

Raymond respects Lisa and wants her to make the most of herself. "She wants to go to school, she wants to be somebody," he says. "And I want her to be somebody!"

Lisa is obviously a bright young woman, something Raymond takes pride in. "She was in the honor class. In the tenth grade, they were going to skip her," he continues. "But then she got pregnant, and she couldn't go anymore. I told her, 'Even though you're pregnant, I'm not going to stop you from going to school. I think you should go back to school.' Other guys don't do that. Other guys say, 'You stay in the house, do what I say!' I used to be like that a little bit, but we had a talk about that, and I can't make all the decisions, you know. She's a woman, she has to make her own decisions. She's not a little girl anymore."

Still somewhat gun-shy about accepting love, Raymond confesses that he has a problem "taking" material things from Lisa. Simple gestures of generosity put him on guard. "Nobody ever gave me nothing," he explains. "So I figure, 'she's trying to give me something—I don't want it.' It's not the trust. I feel guilty. Especially from her."

Lisa wants a more reciprocal relationship, one in which each person can give to the other. "She tells me, 'If you love somebody, it's supposed to be two ways, not just one way.' It's true what she says," he admits.

Both Raymond and Lisa have been able to use their relationship to help each other grow. "My wife changed me a lot," Raymond says. "I showed her and she showed me. Right now she still doesn't know too much, I'm still teaching her. She tells me, 'Well, we *both* don't know too much. You're teaching me but, believe me, I'm teaching you too!' It's true, you know," Raymond adds.

The birth of his daughter has helped him discipline himself. She also brings him a great deal of happiness. "She makes me smile," Raymond says. "She gives me everything. [Having a baby] pushes me more, makes me do what I wanted to do, you know. I figure, I could do it, the baby's there, she's mine, she's part of me now. I don't just love my wife no more, now I love the baby. Now I do for both." It seems that Raymond has been successful in building the family he had to do without for so long.

The fact that Raymond has been able to sustain a four-year relationship with his girlfriend suggests that he will be able to sustain a long-term relationship with his child as well. In addition, there are other things that should increase his chances of becoming a good husband and father.

First, he has been able to use his relationship with his girlfriend as a way of growing and learning. Rather than being threatened by Lisa's intelligence and independence, Raymond has been flexible enough to let her teach him and secure enough to encourage her to develop her own talents. In this way, he resembles several fathers in Part Three.

Equally important, there seem to be many hidden strengths in Raymond's makeup. As a youngster essentially left to raise himself, Raymond has had to learn on his own how to take care of, and care for, others. If he can use these strengths to find a legitimate place for himself in the work force, he—and Lisa and their daughter—should do all right.

PART THREE

■

Devoted Fathers

*I*n spite of their youth and lack of experience, the five teenage fathers described in Part Three are successfully coping with the responsibilities of parenthood. What makes these young men different from the fathers presented in Parts One and Two? Why do they seem better suited to handle the many problems teenage fathers face?

At first glance, the men in this group seem to have greater differences than similarities. Their ethnic, educational, and socioeconomic backgrounds vary. Some live with their children; some do not. All have very different relationships with the mothers of their children. However, there are certain factors that are common to all of them—factors that have influenced their success as fathers.

First, compared to the fathers described in Parts One and Two, the young men in this group are in a better position to support a family. Although Wayne and Gerard are now in a training program getting their high school diplomas, Patrick, Malcolm, and Brian had already graduated and were able to get decent jobs by the time their children were born.

Secondly, the relationships that the fathers in Part Three have with their childrens' mothers tend to be quite different from those of most the young men described earlier. All the fathers in Part Three had long-term relationships (of at least a year) with the mothers of their children well before the girls became pregnant. Most of these relationships seem to be particularly successful, surviving or even improving when the partnership shifted from a romantic involvement to a friendship.

In several of these relationships, the male/female roles are very flexible. Not only are the young men willing to assume the day-to-day duties of raising their children, but they are actually gaining satisfaction from these chores. For their part, the young women involved are generally willing and able to share the financial burden of raising the children. In fact, Brian and his wife have reversed roles completely, with Amy establishing a career and Brian remaining at home to take care of the children.

On the other hand, in Malcolm's case—the one relationship that is not particularly happy—it is precisely the inflexibility of roles and the lack of support from his wife that is the major source of his dissatisfaction.

Because the young men in Part Three seem to feel secure in themselves as males, they are not threatened by the talents and abilities of their partners but instead look to them for support. They are generally proud of their women's intelligence, supportive of their career ambitions, and encourage their partners to develop their own separate identity.

Interestingly, two of these fathers—Malcolm and Brian—consciously used marriage or pregnancy as an escape route from their parents' home. Both Brian and Gerard had alcoholic and abusive fathers, illustrating again that the lack of an adequate role model does not necessarily mean a young man will be a poor father himself.

Finally, although their partners are clearly important to them, these young fathers place their children's welfare above everything else. Without exception, they have a genuine love for their children and thoroughly enjoy interacting with them. As a group, they willingly make enormous sacrifices for their children and, when necessary, fight fierce battles to stay in their lives. If there is any one factor that accounts for their success as parents, it is probably this unselfish devotion.

CHAPTER

9

□

Wayne

*"Get to know your partner. This way, you have
a strong possibility of getting back with her or
being able to do separate things but do
whatever it is you have to do for your baby. If
you know your partner, you can always turn to
her and say, 'Look, I think we need to have a
talk.'"*

When Wayne's girlfriend told him she was going to have a baby,
he didn't know how to react. "I was shocked!" he recalls. "It's not
like I *expected* her to be pregnant, you know. I just didn't know
what to do. It took me by surprise."

Part of him was definitely glad. "In a way, I was happy,
because I love my girl," he says. Wayne had known Yvonne for
three years at that time, and they were very close. "We were like
Bonny and Clyde. I left some of my friends for her. *She* became
my friend. Whatever it is that I wanted to do with my friends, I
could do with her," he adds. "She was there for me. We stayed up

late some nights and played cards. She was like my right-hand man sometimes."

He and Yvonne had talked about having a child. Still, when Yvonne became pregnant, Wayne had doubts about whether it was such a good idea. "Once, I can remember—Yvonne's not going to let me forget it either—I told her maybe we *shouldn't* go through with it," he says. "There was part of me that said it wasn't right. I wouldn't want to put somebody in the world and not be there for them. Why make it harder for the three of us—it's already hard for the two of us."

Now, as the very happy father of a two-year-old girl, he's relieved they decided to have the baby. "I look at it now and I'm completely glad that it happened. It's special, you know…it's special."

Wayne and Yvonne were fortunate in that they had the support of both their families. "Before she was pregnant, I was staying with my girlfriend," Wayne says. "We were like one big happy family, so everything was all right. If they didn't like me, it probably would have been another story."

Nevertheless, Wayne felt scrutinized by Yvonne's parents, as they watched to see how he and Yvonne would handle the situation. "It was a lot of pressure, because they were looking at us like, 'Well, what are you all going to do?' They were seeing, you know, if we were going to go through with it, if we weren't going to go through with it."

Basically, though, Yvonne's parents gave Wayne a lot of emotional support. "They were telling me, 'Well, do the best that you can.' Telling me positive things. And I just took it and followed up," he says.

Wayne's family responded similarly. "They treated my girlfriend as one of ours, one of the family. She stayed at my house, things like that," he recalls. "So it was all right."

But having his father to lean on was especially important to Wayne. "I used to have talks with my father late at night, when

Yvonne was pregnant and even after the baby was born. He used to tell me, 'You have to constantly press yourself now, 'cause this is a serious thing,'" Wayne recalls.

"We've had our differences," Wayne says, speaking of his father. "But we're close. I give him the benefit of the doubt. I always listen, 'cause most of the time, he's right. He opens my eyes to some things I might not open my eyes to on my own. On my own, I probably would be like, 'I'll look at that later.' He tells me, 'Don't sleep. Don't close your eyes. Keep your eyes open, you know, 'cause anything could happen.' He's helping me out by just making me look at those angles."

About the only area in which there was disagreement between Wayne and Yvonne was on the question of marriage. Both she and her mother thought they should get married, but Wayne was reluctant to take that step. "I didn't want to rush into anything," he explains. "I could have just done it, but there was something holding me back—like, see what you can do about this baby first. I felt that if I was to jump into marriage, that'd be two things I'd have to handle. I didn't want to fall on my face. I wanted to take it a step at a time," Wayne adds.

"At first, Yvonne couldn't understand why I didn't just want to say, 'I do,' but I explained that we have to see how far we can get before we jump into another big topic. You know, marriage is a big topic! It's not a girlfriend-boyfriend thing, marriage is much more than that."

Wayne thought he was prepared for having a child because his sister has two children and he had always enjoyed playing with them. But he found there was more to it than he had expected. "Having to get up and check on Yvonne, taking her to the hospital every now and then, having to rush out because she's not feeling well, bringing her certain items from the store she's craving for, dealing with her family while she's pregnant, dealing with my family while she's pregnant, hoping that everything turns out all right..."

Then there was the expense involved. *"Pampers*! Pampers here, Pampers there, constantly saving money so we could have this, have that." Dealing with his little daughter wasn't easy either. "When my daughter was sick, running her to the hospital. Being able to be patient...you know, a lot of things. Especially when it's a newborn!" Wayne exclaims.

"The first year was running around shopping, making sure I got the right clothes...she'd grow out of clothes so quick. I had to learn a lot of things like that, keeping up with her sizes. Taking her on family visits," he adds. "Everywhere I went she was like a prize fish!"

After about a year, however, the couple started to run into difficulties. "When we were together, I don't know, I think we wore it out," Wayne says.

Some of these problems were financial. Wayne had dropped out of high school in his senior year to get a job. Although he worked hard, he didn't make much money. "I wanted to go back to school, but I couldn't because I was still working. She wasn't working, so it was harder with just me, you know," he explains. "Toward the end of that first year, it was best that we separated, because things got hectic as far as being together financially."

But finances weren't the only problem. "Yvonne wanted to go out more after she had the baby. She wanted to run back out and go hang out with her friends," Wayne adds. "I was trying to tell her that might not be the best thing to do right now because we have a newborn."

Wayne misses hanging out with his friends too. "But it's a sacrifice," he says. "It pays off in the end, because once we start getting our daughter settled to the point where we can take a little break, *then* maybe I'll go out a little bit—a *little* bit—not like before, but just to enjoy myself some. Now, it's just constantly going to school, going to work."

After Wayne and Yvonne separated, they started going out with other people. But they made an effort not to let these relationships interfere with their ability to work together as parents. "We made it clear to each other that none of that would have anything to do with what's ours," Wayne says. He told Yvonne, "I don't care what you do with whatever, but keep him away from mine. That's all I ask."

He admits that being with other people could have presented a problem. "But we always try to work things out before they get hectic. We work it out, communicating with each other and all of that."

Unlike many ex-partners, Wayne and Yvonne are good friends. This has helped them to continue to treat each other well and to work together for their daughter, regardless of what else is going on in their lives. "Before she was my girlfriend, I knew her—we were pals. That's another reason why I think she could never turn her back on me, no matter what," Wayne says. "It's not going to help the situation if we turn our backs on each other, because I *know* you. If anything, let's try to keep the problem at a calm pace, instead of making it worse. It's only making it worse by turning your back on someone."

Recently, Yvonne got a job, so some of the financial pressure is off Wayne. Wayne is now back in school, getting his high school diploma. Then, he wants to go to college. "My thing is engineering," he says, "because I like math. I like working with my hands. I'm very good at all of that."

Neither Wayne nor Yvonne is involved with anyone now. "We're leaving that alone," Wayne comments. "She's just trying to get her life together and keep it together, and so am I." Somehow, it wouldn't be surprising if they got back together in the future. "It's like things are mending, the way we want it," Wayne says, smiling.

Like many of the young fathers in this book, Wayne takes great pleasure in his child. "She's like my little pal. She's very playful. She's bright, you know," he says proudly. "Sometimes, I find myself walking down the street and we'll be talking. She's gabbing, but it's talk. I can see that she's going to grow up to be something some day!" Wayne adds. "I'm only trying to keep myself in the right shoes so that if she ever has to turn to me, I can be there like my father was there for me. That's all."

The quality of the relationships in Wayne's life, particularly with his father and his girlfriend, have been instrumental in his ability to be a parent. Of all the young men described in this book, Wayne has the closest relationship with his own father. The value of this relationship in helping him step into his new role as a parent is obvious. Not only has his father provided him with an example of what a father should be, but he was available to guide and support Wayne as he made the transition to fatherhood.

For different reasons, Wayne's ability to build a friendship, as well as a romantic relationship, with his girlfriend has also been important in strengthening the relationship he has with his child. Since both Wayne and Yvonne are committed to working together for the benefit of their child, it is unlikely that he will ever have to fight to see his daughter. Moreover, a child whose parents demonstrate this level of respect for each other is likely to grow up with a good sense of respect for both self and others.

CHAPTER
10

□

Patrick

*"Just watching him everyday, grow a little
more, be able to do more things, watch him
smile...Now he's able to grab things, he's almost
able to sit up. It's just a great feeling to watch
him mature."*

Of all the teenage fathers described in this book, Patrick's
experience has been the least complicated. A number of factors
may have contributed to the relative ease with which he has
assumed the role of father. Because he was nineteen, had
graduated from high school, and had a stable job when his
girlfriend became pregnant, Patrick hasn't faced the extreme
financial pressures that confront some of the other teenage
fathers. Another reason may be the fact he and his girlfriend,
Sharon, are being very careful to take things one step at a time.
Then again, Patrick may just be lucky.

Patrick was at work when Sharon called and told him she
had taken a home pregnancy test and it had been positive. "I
guess the first thing that went through my head was, 'Well, those

things aren't totally right. Why don't we wait till we go to the doctor before we get carried away.'" A week later, the doctor confirmed that Sharon was eight weeks pregnant.

Patrick claims that he and Sharon had generally been very careful about using birth control, with the exception of once or twice when they got a little careless. They didn't think a couple of mistakes would matter too much, however. "I guess we got a little stupid," Patrick says, "because you hear so many stories of how married people have so much trouble and it takes them a couple years or a couple months at least, so we figured the first couple times…"

Knowing their parents would be very upset about the pregnancy, Patrick and Sharon were nervous about telling them. "We planned on telling them but we chickened out a few times," Patrick recalls. "We finally got the nerve to tell her parents. We did it one night when her father wasn't home. I guess I was more scared of him, because you always hear, 'Oh, my little girl,' those kind of stories. So we planned to tell her mother first, then we had her tell her father."

Patrick recalls the incident. "The way we told her, Sharon just gave her the piece of paper from the clinic. She read it and she said, 'What does this mean?' Sharon's like, 'Well, Ma, I think it's pretty self-explanatory. It says…you know.' But her mother kept saying, 'What does this mean?' She just meant she wanted to know what our plans were, but she was in shock. That was pretty scary."

Sharon's father responded better than Patrick had expected. "He handled it real well," Patrick says. "He said, 'These things happen, you've just got to take it in stride. I hope you guys don't plan on getting an abortion.'"

Patrick adds, "We waited a month to two months to tell my parents because my mother was sick and she was going in for surgery, so we didn't want to tell her then. I told her after she was home and feeling better. At first, she was upset—more at herself,

I think. She felt that she didn't do a good job of raising me, because of the mistake I made," he explains. "She said something like, 'Oh, I guess I didn't do a good job of raising him...' and stuff. I told her, 'That's ridiculous! You could be the worst parent or the best parent, kids are going to be kids.'"

As he did with Sharon's family, Patrick let his mother tell his father. "When I told my mother, no one was home except for her and I. After I'd just got done telling her and she was still pretty upset, my father walked in with my brother. He asked what the matter was, because he could tell my mother was upset. A little while later, my mother told him," Patrick says. "She said he was upset too, but I don't know because I didn't really talk to him at that time...I talked to him later on."

It was difficult for Patrick to tell how his father really felt about the situation. "My father's kind of hard to read," Patrick says. "He'll take a situation and make jokes about it, just to lighten everything up, so that's what he did."

Like Sharon's parents, Patrick's family made it clear they were against Sharon having an abortion. "My mother was like, 'Well, at least you're not making two mistakes.' Because both our families are Catholic, so they're totally against it. They're just glad that we didn't do that."

Because of Sharon's plans to go to college, however, she and Patrick briefly considered this option. "Ever since we started seeing each other, which was about a year and a half then, she always told me about wanting to go away to school," Patrick explains. "Getting pregnant kind of ruined that plan. Now she'd have to stay around here to go to school. That's one reason we thought about it," he recalls.

"She was really smart, she made the honor society in high school," Patrick adds. "So, I felt bad that she wasn't going to get a chance to go to the school she really wanted to go to. I would say an abortion crossed both our minds," he concludes, "but in the end, we decided not to."

Although Patrick and Sharon got along well together, prior to the pregnancy they seemed to have had somewhat different expectations about their relationship. Patrick appears to have felt it would come to a natural end when Sharon went off to college.

"If she hadn't been pregnant, I could have seen us being together until the summer. But if she would have went away to school, I think we would have broken up then, but on good terms, because it's kind of hard to still be together while you're so far away. *She* says that we wouldn't have, but I think it would have been better if we did," he comments.

Sharon, on the other hand, clearly wanted a long-term relationship with Patrick. "At first, she wanted to go to college out of state. She was always saying. 'I want to get out of here, to go far away. That's what college is all about.' But then, six months into the relationship, she's talking about schools near here, and how she wouldn't want to go too far away from me. As time went on, we were getting closer and closer, and I guess she didn't want to get too far away," Patrick continues. "I felt bad about that because she was changing her plans just because of me."

Neither Sharon nor Patrick was particularly eager to get married, however, even with a baby on the way. Sharon's parents agreed. "They said we shouldn't get married, because we were still young. I guess they felt that they didn't want us to get married and have the wedding annulled or get divorced in a few years if it didn't work out...Because you're still young and you still haven't seen so many things. You might start regretting things you never got to do and start blaming it on the other person," Patrick says.

Patrick's mother disagreed, at least initially. "My mother wanted us to get married right away," he adds. "I don't know, but sometimes I felt that she cared more about what other people thought, the out-of-wedlock deal. So I think she was more worried about that than about really getting married."

Part of Patrick's reluctance to marry Sharon was financial. "I kept telling my mother, 'Ma, financially it wouldn't benefit us, because of the insurance.' Because mine wouldn't cover it since we'd be getting married after she was already pregnant," Patrick explains. On the other hand, if Sharon remained legally a dependent of her parents, their insurance would cover all medical expenses associated with the baby's birth.

Patrick also worried about who would finance Sharon's college education. "Plus, if we did get married and she went to college, I'm not sure her parents would pay for it. Now, she's still their daughter and it's their responsibility. But if we got married, I don't know if they would say, 'Well, you're married, now you have to pay for it.' And I wouldn't be able to afford it."

They decided the baby should have Patrick's last name, however, even though some of Sharon's relatives wanted the child to use her name. "None of them have children and Sharon's family is four girls," Patrick explains. "I think they were more worried about passing the name down. They probably figured this was their last chance." But Sharon's parents agreed with the couple's decision.

Although they decided not to get married, Patrick did move in with Sharon and her family. As a result, he began to spend almost all his free time with her. In some ways, this was good. "It brought me and Sharon closer together. Before, we saw each other a lot but there was still times, like on the weekends or during the day, I'd spend it with my friends, playing basketball or something. It would be at night when Sharon and I went out," Patrick remembers. "But, after I moved in, we pretty much spent every waking moment together."

Making the adjustment to living together was easier for Sharon than for Patrick. "*She* liked that," Patrick says "I liked it too. But sometimes, I got a little...you just had to get away. *I* felt that way anyway. She said she didn't, but I'm sure I got on her nerves every once in a while."

Patrick also missed doing things with his friends. "There

were times when I just wanted to go and hang out with my friends and be alone for awhile. But Sharon liked it that we spent so much time together, so it was hard for me to get away."

With Sharon pregnant, both she and Patrick stayed home more. "Your lifestyles change," he says. "You get a little more conservative. Sometimes you miss going to all the parties, staying out until all hours of the night. But that's only once in awhile that you get a little depressed. We're both so young," he adds. "Everyone else was still having a gay old time, and we had to slow down a little."

Both Patrick and Sharon had some trepidations about parenthood. "I got scared a lot!" Patrick acknowledges. "So did she. She was more scared about the birth. I was more scared about how well I'd handle it and how good of a father I'd be. That's mainly what I was scared about."

In the five months since his son's birth, Patrick has had plenty of opportunities to see how he'd handle fatherhood, and so far things have gone pretty well. Since he works nights, Patrick took care of the baby during the day so Sharon could go back to high school and graduate.

"It takes a lot of patience," Patrick says. "The all night crying and everything. It's frustrating, but you have to be patient, loving, and caring. It's a lot of work, but it's worth it!"

Recently, Patrick got a promotion at work, so he's better able to handle supporting his son. And, although he's not crazy about the idea, he's decided to go to college himself. "When they promoted me, they said it would be in my best interest if I went back to school, because this is only the first step in management," he says. "Also, it's good to have it because if two people are going for the same spot and one has a degree and the other one doesn't, most likely it'll go to the one with the degree."

The one thing that hasn't worked out for Patrick was living with Sharon and her family. Not long ago, he moved back to his parents' house. "I needed space," he explains. "It's kind of crowded over there. I wasn't used to living in a house with five women. I needed privacy just for myself. It was a different environment, and I guess I didn't like it."

He and Sharon are still together, though. "We're just not living together, because we're both so young. That's kind of a big step at our age to live together," Patrick comments. "It's hard enough when you get married later on in life to adjust, never-mind when we're both teenagers."

He and Sharon plan to get married some time in the future. In the meantime, Patrick sees his son everyday. "He brings a lot of happiness into my life!" Patrick concludes simply.

Patrick's experience as a teenage father has been remarkably similar in many respects to Wayne's. Although these young men come from very different ethnic and socioeconomic back-grounds, the families in which they grew up had at least one thing in common—both included fathers who were present, caring, and who took their role as parents seriously.

Patrick and Wayne are alike in other ways as well. Both young men tend to take things slowly, one step at a time. Although both cared about their girlfriends, they resisted pres-sures to marry before they felt ready—not because they wished to shirk responsibility but because they wanted to get parenting right before they took on the task of being a husband.

Finally, although they didn't marry, each tried living with his girlfriend and found the experience to be too much. To their credit, both couples were able to take a step back and adjust without causing resentment that could have interfered with their ability to be parents.

CHAPTER
11

□

Gerard

*"He doesn't like my girlfriend too much. I guess
he's jealous, because she hugs me and kisses me
and he's like, 'That's <u>my</u> daddy! Leave my daddy
alone!'"*

*I*n his words, Gerard's three-year-old son, Eric, "is my world."
He's had to work hard to maintain his relationship with the boy,
including fighting his ex-girlfriend in court, so when he says "my
life revolves around him," he means it. But Gerard is a father to
more than just his own offspring. He now has a stepson to care
for as well. And he seems to enjoy that almost as much.

Becoming comfortable with being a father has taken time,
however. At fifteen, Gerard's response to his first brush with
parenthood was to run away. "I met this girl and we were seeing
each other for awhile, and she wound up pregnant," he remembers. "She called me and said, 'I'm pregnant.' I was so scared, I
just said, 'Look, it can't be me!' And I hung up the phone."

He was too frightened to say anything to his parents. "I
knew I was going to get into a lot of trouble! You know, fifteen

years old, what are you doing having sex? And now getting this girl pregnant! I just blocked it out," Gerard admits. "I tried to act like there was nothing there. Because at that age, I didn't want the responsibility of a child. 'Responsibility of a child?' I thought. 'I'm still a baby myself!' She hid the pregnancy from her parents for about seven, eight months. I don't know how, but she did. By the time her mother found out, it was too late and she had to have the baby."

Even before the baby was born, her family moved to another city, taking her with them. "It just happened, then she disappeared. I didn't have to worry about it," he says.

Gerard wasn't any happier about the prospect of becoming a father at eighteen. His relationship with his girlfriend, Teresa, was rocky and having a child with her seemed like a bad idea. "Our relationship was based on a lot of fighting—physically, mentally, verbally," Gerard recalls. "Because we were always arguing and fighting, I didn't want the baby. I pushed her towards an abortion. I told her, 'Please, I don't want this baby! We're too young, I don't think we're financially ready, we're still living under your mother's roof, let's get situated so we can take care of it better.'"

Both their mothers agreed. "Her mother told Teresa before, 'You should take birth control.' And when Teresa got pregnant, her mother said, 'I don't think you're ready,'—the same things as me," he recalls.

"My mother didn't really want me to have Eric with Teresa, because she saw us always fighting," Gerard comments. "She said, 'You two are not going to make it together! You shouldn't have this baby! The baby is going to need the mother and the father.'"

But Teresa was determined to have the child. "She's like, 'No, no, no. I'm going to have my baby with or without you.' She was willing to take on the responsibility by herself. So I left her alone. I said, 'Look, I don't want to have nothing to do with this, let's get rid of it, we're too young!' But she stuck by it," Gerard recalls.

"Through her pregnancy, I wasn't there much with her. I moved out and went to stay at my sister's house," he adds.

Gerard strongly suspected that his girlfriend was trying to use the pregnancy to hold onto him. "I didn't want to be with her at the time. But she got pregnant and she forced me to have the baby, thinking, 'Maybe if I have this baby, he'll be with me.'"

He was almost as angry at himself as he was at Teresa. "I felt like I was trapped into having this baby. I felt like I was suckered out. I thought, 'God, why did I let this happen to me?' But at the same time, it was my fault, because I let it happen. I could have used some kind of birth control or something, but you know how things are sometimes when you're young like this. You don't think about that."

If Teresa was trying to use her pregnancy to hold onto Gerard, it worked—at least for a short while. "It pulled me back," Gerard says. "I had to be there for my son, so I quit school and I started working to make some dollars to give to the baby—like a crib, and playpen, and stuff. After seven months, I was with her all the time."

As time passed, Gerard began to look forward to becoming a father. "She was two weeks overdue, and I was *dying* for my son to be born," he recalls. "In the beginning, I didn't want it, but after awhile, he kicks, and you feel him moving inside, and you look forward to having him."

Gerard went through Lamaze classes so he could be present when the baby was born. Watching the actual birth was a little frightening, however. "That was kind of scary—all this blood! I thought, 'Oh, my God, is he all right?' I had an eight pounds, six ounces baby, twenty-two inches long—he was a very big, healthy boy. So I was really happy!"

Unlike many fathers, Gerard provided a lot of the day-to-day care of his son, particularly after he lost his job. "After the second year, he started walking and everything, and I was staying home with him while his mother was working. So, I was all day with him, feeding and changing him and everything. That's why I guess I'm so attached to him."

Gerard and Teresa continued to have trouble getting along, however. Part of the problem was that Gerard wanted to be out in the street more, hanging out. "At the same time, I had a home and a family to take care of," he says. "But I wasn't seeing that at the time. I was getting pulled both ways."

The fighting was also bad for Eric. "My son was always seeing that, and he was always crying and nervous," Gerard says. "We'd get into fights and she'd pick up the baby and put him in between us. And I'd say, 'What are you *doing*?' She was losing it."

Finally, Gerard made a firm decision to go. Teresa didn't give up easily, however, "At the point when I said, 'I don't want to be with you anymore,' she tried to use the baby against me," he recalls angrily. "She said, 'You don't be with me, then you can't see your son.' That's exactly what she did—she used the baby as a tool! It was like, 'Well, I know how to get him! He loves his son, so I'm not going to let him see his son!'" Gerard recalls bitterly.

"She manipulated me to the point that she made me not want to see him," Gerard acknowledges. "She made me not want to be around her, so much that I was like, 'Well, forget him!'" But Gerard caught himself. "I thought, 'Well, I'm not going to make that mistake. Just to forget about the girl, I'm going to forget about my baby? He's going to be mine whether she likes it or not!'"

Unfortunately, the situation escalated further. After one of their fights, Teresa got an order of protection against him. Gerard moved across the street, and, as far as he was concerned, the problem was resolved. For the next two or three months, he didn't bother her and she didn't bother him. During that time, Gerard began going with his current girlfriend, Dolores.

"Then, the day of my birthday, I hear a knock on my door. Me and my girlfriend are getting dressed to go shopping, and I'm all excited," Gerard continues. "And it's the police with the warrant for my arrest. Two months later! She called the police and said, 'I know where he's at. Arrest him!' Because it was my birthday."

This was a turning point for Gerard. Although he had tried to block Teresa and Eric from his mind, "once I saw that she was going all out to hurt me, I said, 'Well, I'm not going to lay down and die for her!'"

Gerard got a lawyer and took Teresa to court. "I fought for visiting rights, and I got it!" he says with a smile. "The judge said, 'He's entitled to see his son two, three days a week, whether you like it or not!'"

Amazingly, since then, Gerard and Teresa have managed to establish a solid friendship that allows them to work together as Eric's parents. "We're the best of friends!" Gerard says. "Now that we're not together, we can communicate, we can hang out, no arguments. The baby needs something, we'll chip in."

Gerard now spends as much time with Eric as he wants. "I keep very close touch with him. Like everyday, I'll go over and pick him up after work or school and then spend two, three hours with him. And on weekends, I'll spend the whole weekend with him," he adds happily.

Teresa has another boyfriend with whom she is expecting a child, and Gerard's girlfriend is also pregnant. Although their new partners are a little threatened by Gerard and Teresa's relationship, Gerard says they have nothing to worry about. "Dolores sometimes thinks I'm fooling around with her, but I'm not," he says. "Believe me, we couldn't get to the point where we could do that again, because it just won't work out. We *both* know that. We're just together for the baby."

The only one who isn't too happy with the arrangement is Eric. Not only is he a little jealous of Dolores, but he clearly wishes his mother and father would get back together. "When I'm at his house, he'll tell me, 'Give Mommy a kiss, give Mommy a kiss.' And we have to explain to him, 'Eric, we can't do that anymore.' And he gets upset about that. Like, he asks me, 'Daddy, stay here, stay the night.' And I say, 'I can't spend the night here.' In reality, all he really wants is for all three of us to be together," Gerard says. "I know that's what he wants, but it just can't be like that anymore."

Eric has had to adjust to two more people in his father's life as well: Dolores's son and Gerard's daughter. To Gerard's surprise, the child he fathered when he was fifteen suddenly reappeared. About six months ago, his old girlfriend returned with their five-year-old daughter, Janelle. Gerard was stunned, but eager to get to know the child. It hasn't been easy for either of them, though.

"When she comes over, she's really shy. She looks scared," he comments. "I try to make her feel at home but it's not so easy, because at the same time, I feel so *funny*. I mean, here's my daughter! I don't know hardly anything about her, so I try to ask her questions and to know her a little better, but...She's my daughter and I'm willing to go all out for her," Gerard says. "If she needs anything, if I've got it, it's hers, no question about it." He'd like to spend more time with Janelle, but her mother hasn't kept her promise to bring the child over, so Gerard isn't sure whether he'll get much of a chance to.

The child Gerard actually lives with, however, is not Eric but David, Dolores's five-year-old son. In the short time they've known each other, Gerard and David have gotten quite close. "He's all right," Gerard says. "We get along pretty good. I play with him, take him to the park, play football and stuff. I care for him," Gerard continues. "Of course, I have no choice! The boy's around me everyday. He's around me more than my own son. So whether you want to or not, you're going to start caring for the kid, you know."

Interestingly, the boy resembles Gerard. "Could you believe, my stepson looks more like me than my real son!" he says. "So, whenever I'm walking in the street, it's, 'Oh, is that your boy? He's so big...' So, he hears a lot, 'Tell your Daddy to come here.'"

At first, this was confusing and awkward for David. "He'd say, 'That's not my Daddy, that's my mother's boyfriend,' or whatever. But that was at the beginning. Now, he'll call me Daddy. The longer the relationship goes on, the closer we get together," Gerard adds.

Integrating their families into one has taken real effort on Gerard and Dolores's part. Like most families composed of siblings, step-siblings, and half-siblings, there are strains in some of the relationships. Occasionally, Dolores complains that Gerard is overprotective of his son when Eric and David are playing, but, as Gerard says, "It's nothing major."

More difficult have been the problems in relating to David's father. "My stepson's father, he really doesn't get along with me because he feels that I'm taking away his son and he can't be around him," Gerard says.

"Well, I'm not telling him not to support his son! He can pass over any kind of money that he wants to support his son. He doesn't give him anything, so what am I going to do, not buy him new sneakers?" Gerard asks. "I have to take care of him, he lives under my roof."

Although he and David are close, Gerard understands just how important it is for a boy to have a relationship with his own father. "My father was an alcoholic and used to beat up my mother, so my mother left him when I was about four or five years old. I didn't have that Daddy kind of companion, so I know what it feels like not to have a father," Gerard recalls.

"She remarried again after I was about seven or eight years old to my stepfather," he continues. "But it wasn't the same. I wanted *my* Daddy, you know. Every few months, when he came along, I was really happy to see him. But you want your father to take you to ball games, and you want to cuddle up in bed with your Daddy and stuff. And I never had that. So, I want to give that to my son," Gerard explains. "With Eric, everything is 'Daddy this...' and 'Daddy that...' and it makes me feel so good! Man, it really makes me feel great!"

Soon, Gerard will have a fourth child calling him Daddy, as he and Dolores are expecting a baby. This is the first time that he'll have become a father on purpose, and he can't wait! "When you actually *plan* to have a baby, it's great!" he says.

Obviously, supporting all these children will require a steady income. Right now, Gerard is finishing high school in a special program. After that, he wants to join the police force. "Several of my friends are officers, and they're pushing me to do it because you make good money and great benefits," he explains. "It's a little dangerous, but hey, you only live once."

Having been through a lot, Gerard has some advice for teenagers who might become parents. "To be honest," he says, "what I would tell young people coming up is to *wait*, to wait as long as they can before they do it. Because it's a *big* step. You cannot imagine how hard it is until you have the baby," Gerard exclaims.

"If you're hungry," he continues, "you can wait awhile before you eat, but that baby doesn't know what wait is. When he's hungry, he wants his bottle, and not to be able to provide that for him, that kills you inside. I'm twenty-one and I can't afford what I want to give my son. And it really bothers me, because you want to give them everything, you want to treat them like kings, and it's hard," he says.

"If you go about it the right way, if you find the right girl, someone you really care about, you'll have a great life and you'll love your kid," Gerard concludes. "But if you're going to jump into something with somebody you really don't know, and you really don't think you're going to last, it's going to cause problems. Because you're going to have to leave your partner and it's going to hurt being separated from your kid." A lesson Gerard learned the hard way!

Gerard's story is perhaps the clearest illustration of the difference age can make in a young man's response to parenthood. At fifteen and sixteen, most teenage boys seem totally overwhelmed at the idea of taking even limited responsibility for a child. Like Gerard and Kenton, they often try to disassociate themselves completely from both the child and the child's mother. By eighteen or nineteen, however, many of the same young men feel a responsibility toward the child, even when they may not want the baby.

Gerard is also an example of how hard some adolescent fathers will fight to have a relationship with their children and how important continued contact is in sustaining that relationship. As Gerard points out, it is difficult not to become attached to a child you live with, even if it isn't your own. On the other hand, building a relationship with your own child after years of having no contact is very difficult.

Finally, Gerard and Dolores's success in handling the intricacies of a combined family is remarkable. Many older couples would be unable to cope with the often conflicting interests and loyalties involved in this situation. It may have taken him a few years, but it appears that Gerard is a "natural" father if there ever was one.

CHAPTER

12

□

Malcolm

*"The pressure is incredible. I wish I could just
leave and start over. That's a fantasy I know
and I don't really mean it, but it does wear on
you."*

*I*n many respects, twenty-two-year-old Malcolm's story is a very
traditional one. When he graduated from high school at age
eighteen, he and his girlfriend, Debbie, got married. In less than a
year, they had become the parents of a son. On the surface, they
may look like the all-American family. For Malcolm, however,
there's a lot of disappointment and unhappiness underneath.

In retrospect, Malcolm isn't quite sure why he decided to
get married. "I think I wanted to get on with life like my brothers
and sisters," he says. "I was uncomfortable being the only one left
at home with my mother. Besides, I had no plans to go to college
or anything, so the natural step for me seemed to be marriage
and my own family."

Somehow, getting an apartment by himself seemed too
threatening at the time. "I thought about that," Malcolm says, "but

the thought of going out on my own seemed impossible to me then. Now, of course, I realize I could have handled it. I probably should have gone that route first, because I know I missed out on a lot of things—bachelor things," he says with regret. "My home growing up was very strict. Being the baby of seven kids, I was spoiled crazy. But I guess I never had any freedom of my own. I'm sorry about that."

Malcolm and Debbie had talked about having children. "But it was more like, 'When we decide to have kids...' and 'Someday we'll have children,'" he says. "I wanted to be in my late twenties, maybe my thirties. I thought I was being responsible about it. We were supposed to take the first couple of years and get ourselves set up," Malcolm recalls. "We really *did* have plans. I did at least. She had her own set of plans, I guess." Those plans included getting pregnant as soon as possible.

There is no doubt in Malcolm's mind that his wife purposefully deceived him to do this. "Oh yeah! I think that's really obvious," he says. "I guess I'm a fool," Malcolm adds , ruefully. "I thought she was—she *said* she was —on the pill. But I never saw her take them. I was stupid, I know."

Malcolm's immediate reaction to the pregnancy was anger. "I was really mad that she lied to me," he says. "I was also real worried—you know—scared! Like, 'How the hell are we going to survive!' I didn't feel old enough to be a father and, between you and me, I thought Debbie was still a little girl. I was more afraid of her being a mother."

A view of the future flashed in front of him, and Malcolm didn't like the picture at all. "I *knew*, I *knew* at that point how it was going to be!" he recalls angrily. "I could see it! She was going to have a baby and we'd all have to pay attention to her. And I'd have to 'take care' of everything. Oh, man! It was weird too, because here we're only married for a couple of months, right? I'm all big-headed because I'm a married man with a fine wife.

And then, BOOM! Things change! I guess my whole life just changed right then," he adds sadly.

Malcolm also believes Debbie made sure he'd be in no position to even suggest an abortion. "Are you kidding?" he asks. "With my family, forget about it! Plus, Debbie told everybody right away. I don't think I was the first to find out. My mother and sisters knew right away. And, of course, she told her mother. The whole world knew I was going to be a father. I couldn't come out and say, 'Well, I don't think this is the right time,' or anything. People were patting me on the back and I was still trying to make sense of it. It wasn't supposed to happen, at least not that fast."

Malcolm thinks his mother understood his predicament. "My mother spoke to me a couple of times by herself, and I think she wished it wasn't like that," he remembers. "I know she thought I was too young. But what's she going to say? You've got to do what's right at that point. I mean, *she* taught me that! You can't run from it. You've got to make the best out of the situation."

Debbie loved being the center of attention. "She really demanded attention," Malcolm comments, " and that was hard to deal with. The families didn't help either because everybody was acting like this was the most exciting thing. Oh, and she spent *a lot* of money on the baby."

Malcolm wasn't sure how to respond to Debbie because he didn't know what to expect from a pregnant woman. "She couldn't wake up in the morning, she was so tired," Malcolm says. "I thought she was being lazy at first. She started calling in sick a couple of times a week once she was six months pregnant." Already worried about their rising expenses, Malcolm was concerned that Debbie would get fired. "I thought, 'Damn! She's going to lose her job!' But then I thought, 'I better take it easy, maybe she really is sick.'"

As the pregnancy progressed, Malcolm began to feel he

should handle Debbie with kid gloves. "You get a little scared being the guy, because you're always on the outside. You never know what's going to happen next," he explains.

"And women! They tell these horror stories about being pregnant. My sister was the worst. She liked to psych me out all the time. They make you feel like you've got to treat your woman like china or you're going to hurt her and the baby."

As the pressure began to build, Malcolm looked for an escape. "I started to drink," he recalls. "I've stopped now, but at the time, I'd use any excuse to go hang out with the guys. I was running away from the problem, I guess, but I didn't know what else to do."

If he was hoping Debbie might realize he was having trouble coping, he was mistaken. "It was like she didn't notice I was drinking and stuff," Malcolm says, describing her reaction. "I don't know, maybe that's why I stopped."

When Debbie went into labor, though, Malcolm acted like a typical first-time father. "I was very excited and proud! For the first time, I was really happy! I couldn't wait to see what it was, a boy or a girl," he remembers.

"I told everybody I worked with and anybody who'd listen, 'I'm going to have a baby! I'm going to have a baby!' I don't remember how I got to the hospital. All I know is that I was there."

In the waiting room with his family, he began to worry. "It seemed like a long time and I started to panic, but everybody said it was fairly fast for a first baby. It took five hours." Malcolm and Debbie named their son Benjamin, after her father.

This seems to have been the high point of parenthood for Malcolm. From then on, things got even more difficult. "When we got married, we both had jobs and that's what our plan was. We figured we could make it if we both brought home paychecks and saved a little. That all changed when Benjamin was born," he says.

"I knew Debbie would be on a leave of absence from work. But, I mean, she *left*! She won't go back to work because she's got this little girl's fantasy of staying home with the baby and being a little Suzy Creamcheese. I'm working my ass off and she's not contributing anything to us financially. She knows we can't keep going on like this, but she hopes I'm going to be so scared that I'll get better and better jobs," he adds. "I'm not sure I can."

It's hard to imagine how much more scared Malcolm could get. "She wants to move near where my brother and sister live. She wants a car. She always needs clothes. She's living in a dream world! I only make twenty four thousands dollars. How can I buy a house and a car on that? I can't!"

Benjamin is now four years old and Debbie's mother has offered to keep him during the day so that Debbie can return to work. "But Debbie doesn't *want* to work!" Malcolm says. "She says it's not good for the baby. I think he's her excuse. I think either she's just lazy and likes the arrangement or she's afraid of working. We've talked about it," Malcolm adds, "but she takes on this Mother Superior attitude, like I'm wrong for wanting her to work."

The hurt, disappointment, and sense of betrayal Malcolm feels are obvious. "I thought when we got married that Debbie and I would work out anything that came up together, that it would be easier. But sometimes, Debbie is my biggest problem. It's like I have to take care of two other people," he says.

"I feel like she's thrown the whole burden on me. I sound like a kid, but I don't think it's fair. We were supposed to have a partnership. I was supposed to be able to depend on her as much as she depends on me."

Struggling to juggle his responsibilities, Malcolm is not sure that he's doing the right things as a father. "I always look at other guys who are older," he says, "and I say, 'Do I do that? Should I act like that?' I'm definitely not sure of how to handle everything," he adds. "I know it comes with time. I just hope I don't make too many mistakes!"

Malcolm's relationship with his wife contrasts dramatically with the relationships other fathers in Part Three have with their children's mothers. Unlike their relationships, Malcolm's marriage is characterized by rigid roles and a division of labor that places the entire financial burden on him. Moreover, he doesn't seem to receive the emotional support in trying to fill the role of breadwinner that the other young men get from their partners. In fact, if he is right about Debbie's motives, his relationship with her can hardly be considered to be a partnership in any sense of the word. Perhaps the saddest aspect of Malcolm's situation, however, is that he seems too stressed to enjoy even his child.

CHAPTER
13

□

Brian

*"He hit me a lot and he hit my mom... I was
afraid the moment I became a father I'd turn
into my father. It was frightening."*

*I*f Malcolm's marriage typifies the conventional relationship
between husband and wife, then Brian's is certainly the least
traditional. Married at eighteen and the father of two daughters,
Brian has successfully exchanged roles with his wife, Amy. He is
now a full-time homemaker and Amy, who continued her
education throughout both pregnancies, has a high-powered
career. The arrangement suits them both perfectly.

Warm and charming, with a witty sense of humor, Brian is
thrilled with his life as a husband and father. He is proud of his
ability to be a nurturing caretaker and truly loves the process of
raising his daughters. "I would kill for those girls," Brian says half
in jest. "I love getting up in the morning and getting them
dressed. Feeding them, walking them..."

Listening to Brian, it's hard to believe that he did not grow
up in an environment like the one he provides for his own

children. Brian's childhood was anything but nurturing, however. "It wasn't your typical American family, if you follow me," Brian says. "My father drank a lot and was a tyrant. He made life for me, my mom, and my brothers a living hell. He was just a miserable bastard, angry because no one liked him. I don't think he'd know how to behave like a real family. But something sick inside him thought he deserves one...and it was our fault it wasn't there," Brian recalls bitterly.

"He took it out on me mostly. He didn't really hurt us physically," Brian says, "but after awhile that kind of treatment wears you out."

His father's behavior made it impossible for Brian to bring friends to the house. "My friends thought he was crazy. No one ever wanted to come to the house. He'd throw them out! Right like that! He'd say, 'Get the—out of my house!'" Brian recounts in disbelief.

Not surprisingly, both Brian's older brothers left the house as soon as possible. "My older brother Larry went into the armed forces right out of high school. So you know it was because of my dad. And Mike—he's two years older than me—he was living with some guys when he was seventeen." This left Brian and his mother to face his father's tirades alone. "My brothers left. And my mother and I hated him," he says.

Fortunately, when he was sixteen, Brian met Amy, and his relationship with her provided a welcome relief from the chaos at home. Although Amy was two years younger, he was able to talk with her and vent some of his anger and frustration. Brian credits her for helping him through a lot of the rough times with his father.

When he was eighteen, Amy became pregnant. Brian was both "scared to death and very happy!" "I finally had a reason to move on with my life," he explains. "I didn't think I could be a father or husband, but I definitely knew I couldn't take my father anymore."

Since Brian and Amy are Catholic, neither one of them considered getting an abortion. "She thinks, and so do I, that if you get pregnant, that's it. *You* are going to have a baby. We had no choice. We wouldn't have done it any differently, believe me," Brian recalls.

"The only way her parents would allow us to get married was if I had a good job and could support her," he continues. Because the police force was one of the few places where he could earn an income that would be adequate for himself, Amy, and a baby, Brian decided to become a cop.

Although Brian had graduated from high school by this time, Amy was still in her junior year. Unfortunately, she had to quit when her pregnancy became obvious. Determined to graduate, however, she continued to study with her teachers after school.

Brian took to marriage easily. "I figured I could hang in as a husband pretty good after awhile. I liked being married," he says. But his upbringing had left him with some scars that surfaced early in Amy's first pregnancy. "Even to the last day before she gave birth, I had nightmares...of killing the kid or something. I mean by accident of course! I was scared I'd hurt it or do something messed up to hurt it. Oh yeah—then I was afraid the baby would be born with something wrong with it. I had nightmares all the time."

Brian never told Amy about his nightmares, but he believes he understands what was going on for him at that time. "I think they [the nightmares] were very obvious," he says. "I was scared. I grew up with a jerk as a father figure, and I was afraid I wouldn't know how to be a father myself."

There were other things to worry about as well. "The responsibility is overwhelming too," Brian adds. "Can you pay the bills? Will your wife always love you? Can you handle everything without going crazy or just skipping town?"

Brian had no intention of skipping town. He is quite proud of his ability to be a father, especially now that he has the experience of two children. "I'm getting better all the time!" he declares. "With the first, I was afraid to change her diapers. Afraid I'd drop her. But by the time the second came around, I was very comfortable."

Soon after Brian's second daughter was born, he was shot in the line of duty. Brian and Amy decided it was time to make some radical changes. While he had never enjoyed his job, Amy had gotten a Masters degree in the interim and wanted a career. It seemed to make more sense for him to stay home with the children while she worked.

The new arrangement thrilled Amy. "Amy is smart. She likes to work. She's ambitious and she expects to make it big! Everyone knew that she'd go far on her own," Brian says.

"As it turns out, I'm home with the girls and she's supporting all of us. But I think everyone is happy about that. Her and her parents."

How does Brian feel he's doing? "Mr. Mom, right?" he jokes, but it's apparent that he loves the job. "I like being with the kids during the day. I don't do everything right. Amy says I spoil them. But I do love them desperately. And I'd rather stay home with them and my wife than hang out. I've been such a homebody for the last so many years that I can't remember that last time I went out without them, or at least Amy."

His wife clearly approves of the job he's doing. "I think she depends on me to love the girls a lot and to watch over them. I'm very protective. I don't think I'm crazy about it or anything but if I take them to the park, I watch them. I'm not easily distracted. I don't get bored with them either. I think some fathers do get bored. They need to get away from their kids. I'm the opposite."

Brian has very strong feelings about fatherhood, especially teenage fathers. When asked what characteristics he feels are important in a young man, he replies, "Someone who is honest with himself. A guy who sees that what he's getting into isn't always a bed of roses. Someone who also doesn't want or expect anything from his relationships with his kids," he adds. "My dad expected me to worship him. That either happens or it doesn't," he continues. "The best dads don't think about themselves, they think about their kids, and the kids pick up on that."

Brian recalls how his priorities have changed since he was an adolescent. "You've got all these weird things on your mind when you're a teenager," he comments. "I kept thinking when my wife was pregnant that sex wouldn't be any fun anymore. Well, you know, after awhile the baby and her health are just more important than when the next time you have sex is."

He also knows how financial pressures can seem to take the pleasure out of life. "Young guys are at a disadvantage when it comes to supporting their families," he says. "I'm a good example of that. My wife likes to work and she expects to be successful. But not all women want that, especially if they have children. Many girls expect their man to take care of them and their children. I could barely afford to take care of my family," he admits. "I didn't *choose* a career, it was a necessity. Young guys don't see how disappointed they're going to be. When you're a young guy with a wife and baby and you have to work at something you hate because there just isn't any choice, it's not easy."

From an unhappy adolescent fleeing a chaotic home, Brian has successfully matured to a responsible adult and parent. Yet he refuses to take the credit himself. "I'm the one who is lucky," he says, smiling. "I'm the most happy I've ever been! I've never felt so safe or loved before in my life. Amy and the girls are responsible for that."

Both Malcolm and Brian used marriage as a way of leaving their parents' houses, a behavior usually thought to be more typical of young women than young men. It's interesting that neither seemed able to leave on their own, in spite of the fact that both were capable of taking responsibility for a wife and children.

Both young men have felt crushed by having to carry the sole financial responsibility for a family. With a willing partner and a flexible relationship, however, Brian has been able to find a solution that makes everyone happy.

Programs for Teenage Fathers

As the young men in this book illustrate, teenage fathers are as diverse a group as older fathers. Although some have little or no interest in their children, many others are eager to assume the responsibilities of being a father. The obstacles facing teenage fathers are significant, however, and they can use all the help they can get. With this in mind, a number of agencies have recently begun to develop programs to assist young men in being parents to their children.

The YM/YWCA in several cities has initiated programs for teenage fathers. These programs provide young men with help in finishing school and finding employment. Frequently these programs also include support groups, in which adolescent fathers can talk about the problems they face with their parents, their children's mothers, and their children.

Job-training programs for teenage parents, while generally utilized by young mothers, usually welcome fathers as well. Another resource that is sometimes overlooked by a young man is the social worker assigned to the mother of his child. The social worker can frequently be helpful in directing the young father to a program geared to his specific needs.

Unfortunately, the availability of programs can fluctuate from year to year, with new programs springing up while others are discontinued. Ministers, school guidance counselors, drug abuse counselors, and Head Start personnel are also good sources of current information. If one of these people doesn't know, ask the next. You deserve the help!

Further Reading

Dash, Leon. *When Children Want Children: An Inside Look at the Crisis of Teenage Parenthood.* New York: Viking-Penguin, 1990.

Levant, Ronald. *Between Father and Child: How to Become the Father You Want to Be.* New York: Viking-Penguin, 1991.

Lindsay, Jeanne Warren. *Teens Look at Marriage: Rainbows, Roles, and Reality.* Buena Park, CA.: Morning Glory Press, 1985.

——————. *Teens Parenting—Your Baby's First Year: A How-to-Parent Book Especially for Teenage Parents.* Buena Park, CA.: Morning Glory Press, 1991.

Miner, Jane C. *Young Parents.* New York: Julian Messner, 1985.

Pennetti, Michael. *Coping with School Age Fatherhood.* New York: The Rosen Publishing Group, 1988.

Robinson, Bryan E. *Teenage Fathers.* New York: The Free Press, 1987.

Sayers, Robert. *Fathering: It's Not the Same.* Larkspur, CA.: The Nurtury Family School, 1983.

Schnell, Barry T. *The Teenage Parent's Child Support Guide.* Newark, DE.: Consumer Awareness Learning Laboratory, 1988.

Silverstein, Herma. *Teen Guide to Single Parenting.* New York: Franklin Watts, 1989.

INDEX

Acknowledgments

Although we are technically the authors, in a very real sense this book was written by the thirteen young men who were willing to share their experiences of fatherhood with us. For reasons of confidentiality, we cannot acknowledge them by name. However, we can say, "You know who you are and, to you all, many thanks!"

In addition, there were several professionals whose insights were invaluable to us in understanding the pressures faced by young fathers as they attempt to cope with parenthood. In particular, we would like to thank Ellen Dorsey, Anita Moses, Clarence Berry, Loretta Misurac, C.S.W., the Educational Planning Institute, and the New York YWCA Teen Parent Program.

About the Authors

KAREN GRAVELLE, PH.D., M.S.W., is a freelance writer and photographer specializing in books for adolescents. Her previous books include TEENAGERS FACE TO FACE WITH CANCER, TEENAGERS FACE TO FACE WITH BEREAVEMENT, and UNDERSTANDING BIRTH DEFECTS, as well as several animal books for children. Ms. Gravelle lives in New York City.

LESLIE PETERSON, once a teenage parent herself, is now a freelance writer and financial professional residing in New York City.